The Chronicles of Lila Ray:

IF I HAD ONE CHANCE TO TELL YOU SOMETHING

M. N. Walters

ISBN: 9798218312350

Book design and cover illustration by Aura Lewis

The joy and light of my life.
To my husband with love.
To my family with love.
Thank you for always believing in me and encouraging me.
Thanks for cheering me on.
I'm thankful for all of you.
Russell, Mom, Dad, Moise, I love you all.

To my loved ones who went before me, you'll always be a part
of me, a part of my growing up and a part of me. I miss you.
I cherished every memory.

This book is dedicated to anyone who ever had a dream.
To anyone who never felt good enough, you are someone.

Believe. Never give up. Be you. Be inspired.

Chapter 1

I got up and got ready for the day. Another great day and I am excited to see what it brings. I wrote a journal entry of sorts. This is the story of a girl named Lila Ray (that's me). It's a story about the people I meet who make me think. Have you ever thought about stereotypes? What do they mean? Where do they come from and why? Are they true or do we make them true? These are all things that I think about because who doesn't judge, and, well, there are so many people in the world who have different opinions, backgrounds, likes, dislikes, and looks. This is an account of what I see and life as I know it. The story of the people I meet, how they feel, what they go through, and the situations I find myself in and how I react to them. This is the story of two people who became my best friends: Adam and Tara. People like to think of me as some sort of heroine, and I like to be when I can, but Adam is the real hero. This is about them.

I'm twenty-three years old. Traveling is what I do; it's innate, and I love meeting people and hearing their stories. I see and hear a lot. I see discrimination, I see judgments, I see hurt and broken people, I see bad in the world, and I see good in the world. I see people made whole again, and I see people with pure goodness time and time again. I know I can learn so much from knowing these people, listening, and being myself. Welcome to this story.

I got my outfit ready for work and put on my colorful above-the-ankle socks, grabbed my sunglasses, and hit the road. It was a beautiful, warm, sunny day. The flowers, trees, and plants were shining.

"Hey Jesse," I shouted to my neighbor as he stood

behind his fence with his dog.

"Hey Lila Ray," he shouted, "stay out of trouble."

"I'll try, but I can't make any promises," I said. "I'm a rebel with a cause, yes with a cause!"

When I got to work, I saw Adam preparing to serve a new table of customers who had just come in. Adam is my awesome coworker. He is super cool. We work at De La Lina. It's an upscale restaurant with diverse cuisine. The beautiful, exquisite ambiance and design are unique, elegant, and inviting. The location is in Monterey, California, in the Big Sur region. That's where I grew up: the Golden State. The land of palm trees and redwoods.

Adam was born in Colorado but moved here when he was little and would visit Colorado with his family from time to time. Adam is built, with a muscular frame. He's stylish and has light, bright blue eyes, and blondish brown hair. He always wears a smile with his blondish-brown beard.

I saw Adam walk over to a table of six people, some of whom were glaring at him with looks of disgust. He spoke with kindness and professionalism. The people reluctantly told him they weren't ready yet.

"No worries. Take your time," he said. "I'll bring over some water for the table." They whispered as he walked away. Soon after, one lady at the table got up and approached the manager. As Adam walked back with the waters for the table, the people had all moved to Delilah's section. I saw the look of disappointment and confusion on Adam's face as he walked away to help another table. I stood and observed for a moment and heard the whispers of the table.

"I don't want a guy covered in tattoos to serve us," one customer said.

Another chimed in, "Who knows what he was doing

before he came in today. Maybe those weren't the only needles he's ever used. He's probably involved in criminality or is unsanitary."

Adam has some tattoos on his neck, hands, fingers, two arm sleeves, and one full-leg sleeve. The other leg has two tattoos below the knee and one above, but the rest is skin.

"What ridiculous person would want all of that? I can't understand why someone would fathom having so many tattoos. To me it's just unnecessary. He's probably a degenerate or been to jail. I'm sure he's not a good person," one of the diners said.

"Too bad," another said, "he's a really good-looking guy. He looks like he is a cross between a model, a rock star, and a gym trainer."

"Who cares," said another, "it looks fine, let him be. To each their own. What does it have to do with his service? I don't see how it correlates."

Just then I glanced over at Adam. I could tell by the expression on his face that he'd heard what they'd said. He went on with his duties for the night with grace, though. I told myself that I would ask him about it when we got off. Adam was always friendly and would wave at me.

Two hours later, when we finished up and started walking to our cars in the parking lot, I asked him if we could talk.

"Sure," he said.

"I saw what happened and it wasn't right."

"I'm pretty used to it," he said with a shrug.

"It's completely messed up that people can judge someone based on their appearance without even knowing them," I said.

Adam nodded in agreement.

"It happens, and I know that some people have those perceptions, but I don't let it get to me too much. I can't control other people's perceptions. I don't get it though. People should treat everyone with respect and dignity. Not judge a book by its cover or condemn. It's not like having tattoos affects or limits my ability to work and be a good employee. It hasn't changed who I am as a person."

"I completely agree with you Adam, and it's good that one at that table wasn't like that." Simultaneously an older lady in the parking lot dropped her bags on the ground. Adam went over to pick them up for her. "Get away from me," she said. "I don't need help from someone like you."

I stepped in quickly. "What do you mean *someone like him?*"

"Look at him," she said. "He is not a sensible young man with those tattoos. He destroyed his natural skin. He's probably up to no good. A rebellious generation." She got in her car and slammed the door shut as she muttered. I looked over to Adam.

"I'll catch you tomorrow, Lila," he said. I could see the disbelief and hurt in his face.

"Wait, do you want to talk about what happened?" I asked.

"Some people are ignorant and won't change," he said.

I told him that having those perceptions is sad because he is such a nice, respectful, and caring guy. I asked him to tell me a bit about it.

"I started getting tattoos when I was nineteen because they intrigued me, and I liked them," Adam said. He just had the idea to start with two, and then his interest grew from there, and the people at the shop became like a second family to him. He's twenty-eight now. He is into art, and having tattoos allows for his artistic expression. He likes the meaning behind his tattoos.

I have no tattoos, but working with Adam helped me to see that it doesn't matter if you do or you don't, but it does matter how you treat people. Sometimes our brains see and judge people for different things, and I reflected on that for a moment. *Is it learned?* I wondered.

Adam is someone that is easy to be drawn to because he is so captivating and caring to others. He engages in conversation and makes a point of relating to almost anyone who he talks to. He truly treats people the way that he wants to be treated, but some people can't look past his exterior and see into his soul and heart. It wasn't something that we had spoken about before tonight.

"It hurts sometimes," Adam said. "It's fine if people don't like tattoos or don't want them for themselves, but for them to say all those things about my character and who I am as a person isn't right, and it's not who I am. Getting judged and having assumptions made about you comes with the territory though."

He told me that people have assumed certain things about him from his past or that he would do certain things because he has tattoos, and the assumptions that people make about him are often wrong. He notices it when he walks into a restaurant, wondering whether they would accept him, or when people ask him about what he does for work. Hearing what Adam felt and seeing what he went through that night caused me to reflect on something that I've seen but never really put much thought into. Stereotypes and perceptions are so real. People make judgments and biases every day. Adam knows about the stereotypes for tattooed people, such as being untrustworthy or irresponsible, doing drugs, taking dangerous risks, having anything go, a lack of morals, and potential job rejection.

I wonder how I can change them and have people see through a different lens. Having tattoos didn't change Adam's character, values, or beliefs. He is still a person first, and there is more to who he is beneath his skin.

The people who dismissed Adam as their waiter came out and saw us in the parking lot. A couple of them still gave looks of disgust and dismay, but one guy in the group approached Adam and said, "For what it's worth, I can tell that you're a good guy."

"Thanks, man," Adam said. Adam and the man gave each other a nod as the man went on his way.

I asked Adam if we could hang out soon. He intrigued me and I wanted to get to know him better for who he was underneath the tattoos and more than the hi and bye of acquaintances or small talk. I admired how he handled situations with resiliency.

The next day Adam, another coworker, and I went to the beach. I learned just how adventurous, fun, and thrilling Adam is. I told him that while I never thought too much about tattoos—I only really knew people who had a couple or a few tattoos. Knowing someone like him who has so many was different for me. Maybe I had a subconscious idea about the type of person that would have so many but working with him and seeing his character really shifted that for me completely. Outside appearance has nothing to do with the type of person someone is, and one size does not fit all.

It reminded me of the Bible verse that says, "Man looks at the outward appearance, but God looks at the heart." It made me think about how people including myself look on the outside, but God sees beyond that and knows us more than we even know. I wanted to be more like God. I never thought badly or much about Adam for having tattoos, and I never judged his character, but maybe I didn't realize what knowing someone who looked like that would feel like. He really enthralls me. It is still sort of different yet becoming so popular. Many like and accept it.

Still, I think tattoos give some people a perception and prejudgment, and I know that some people don't like tattoos or may wonder why he is basically covered in them. Sometimes, like with Adam, the judgment is totally wrong and off. He doesn't deserve the treatment that he got, that I am sure of, and he is fully aware of the judgments that some people think about him.

The next day at work, Adam was back serving tables. The customers from the other day came in, and Adam turned to me and said, "You can't win them all," with a grin.

"Are you going to take that table?" I asked.

"I'll try," Adam said with a playful grin.

"It's a new day," I said as he rushed off.

"Hi, I'm Adam, I'm going to be your server today. Can I get you started with anything?" he asked them.

Jodi, one of the managers, came over. "Adam is the best," she said.

The people shrugged and gave him their orders but with obvious reluctance. I heard the man that spoke to him in the parking lot the other day say to his table, "Look, he's fine, and our food will be fine."

Adam served them with grace, professionalism, and courtesy despite how they treated him in the last interaction. Where I am positioned in the room as a hostess gives me a great spot to see everything that is happening. It gives me interesting interactions with different people as well who I get to meet and be kind to.

As he walked towards me, Adam gave me a look, you know, that here goes nothing look, and I gave him a sideways smile and whispered, "You got this", as he walked by. I watched as he brought water and appetizers to their table.

"Did you wash your hands?" one lady asked him. "I know you can't wash the filth off from altering your skin, but you can at least wash your drug-dirty hands," she whispered to the man next to her right in front of Adam."

I stood there taken aback. Stereotypes. I figured that Adam would be appalled.

I watched him reply. "You know what, ma'am? I don't do drugs, and I have washed my hands frequently throughout my shift. Not only is hygiene important to me, but so are the people that I serve."

She scoffed at him. "I don't believe it. If you don't care about damaging your skin with those needles and ink, you probably don't care about cleanliness and hygiene. Have you been to jail?" she asked.

Mike, the head manager, came over and asked the table if there was a problem. The man who had commented to Adam in the parking lot said, "No, we're fine," but one lady said that she wasn't happy with the waiter that they got yet again. "Is everything okay with the service you are receiving today?" Mike asked. "His appearance is not pleasing to me," the unhappy woman scoffed, while the rest of the group sat quietly.

"There are no laws against tattoo discrimination," Mike said, "and I know that Adam made the choice to get tattoos on his body, which we accept here, but you also have the choice right now to treat him like a human being and with the respect and courtesy that I have seen him giving you, which is what we expect at this restaurant from our employees. He is one of my best waiters. As a customer we want to serve you and allow you to have a comfortable and enjoyable dinner experience, and I don't think that his tattoos will take that away from you."

"He looks unprofessional, and I think he has some kind of issue getting all those tattoos," the woman said.

Meanwhile, another hostess who heard told me, "What is unprofessional is turning someone down and rejecting them for tattoos." She rolled her eyes and sighed.

"Ma'am, I'm sorry that you feel that way. That's unfortunate. Let me know if there is anything I can do to help," Mike said.

"Is she serious?" Mike rhetorically looked at me and asked about the diner as he turned his head to the side and widened his eyes. He went back over to the table.

The man in the group that had spoken to Adam jumped in. "It is fine, we will stay here," he said. "It is busy anyway, and we don't need to cause any more trouble. This conversation is loud and he's hearing it all."

"Hey Adam, hey man, are you good with serving this table because I can put you with another table that would love and appreciate to have your service?" asked Mike as they stepped back. "I'm good; if this is the last complaint, I can put it behind me. I just want to do what I do which is serve the customers respectfully and elevate their experience here in the short time I have with them," Adam said.

Meanwhile, I was processing everything that I was seeing and hearing.

"Adam," I said, "are you okay?"

"Just another day, Lila, it happens," he said.

"I get that with such highly visible tattoos some people could feel taken aback or hold on to traditional views about your body, or not like your choice of tattoos, but what really bothers me is the lack of respect and understanding that you get treated with," I said. "It was your choice to get tattoos, and you treat all your customers with respect and poise. You always want to help them to have a great restaurant experience and keep coming back, so to see you get treated like this really irks me."

"Thanks Lila! It really means a lot. I'd be lying if I said that I never got bothered with being judged. What's helped me is just changing what I think about it."

Moments like these remind me of my old WWJD bracelet that I had growing up that stood for *What Would Jesus Do?* All I can think to do is make Adam feel worthy because I believe that everyone is. I believe that he is. Sometimes I am also not sure what to say or ask because I don't want to offend him or be another person who makes it seem like his tattoos are a big deal to me or how I see him. I give people respect and Adam has never given me a reason not to.

Shortly after, Adam got a table with a couple. The man and the woman at the table were kind to him. They were your typical good customers who show mutual respect for the server. They didn't appear to judge him in any way and were polite when they were ordering. I could tell that Adam was relieved to have friendly and decent customers. They didn't say a word about his tattoos, almost like they didn't see them. They did, but they did not acknowledge them. They made small talk.

His tattoos are not intimidating or scary, but there are a lot, and some are colorful so they stand out. I know some may say, well, he wouldn't get this treatment if he didn't get tattoos, but I say, well, he did, and it has caused me to really think about people's differences, views, outlooks, and the way that we treat other people.

As the night went on some teenagers came in to eat and they asked if they could have Adam as their server.

"Good evening guys, I'm Adam, what can I get you?" He asked.

"We'll have two iced teas and a lemonade please," one of them replied.

"Hey, man, those tattoos are dope. How old were you when you first got one?" One of the boys asked.

"I was 19 when I started and it's been quite a journey, and a lot of time in and out of the shop I go to," Adam replied.

"Quick question, if you don't mind," the boy said.

"Go ahead," Adam said.

"When did you get the one with the clock and what made you want that one?" the boy asked.

"I got that one a few years ago, and it represents time being universal. It never stops or goes back, it's constant so we have to appreciate it and make the most of it," Adam answered.

They were enthralled. They smiled and laughed with Adam as he served them during their dinner and wrapped the night up.

This night ended on a good note, and it gave me a good feeling because I get joy from seeing others be happy and when people treat others with compassion. It's the small things in life that warm my heart. It really got me thinking, if there are ten good customers and one bad one, the bad one is the one that we could be left thinking about and questioning later. With that, there are also positive and regular customers too, which always feels good, but for some reason, bad, rude, hurtful, and negative comments tend to stand out in our minds and affect us more.

I hope my presence and support for him also helps. I don't have to have tattoos to be able to support and respect him.

I also want to have empathy. The world and people are different yet so similar in so many ways. We are human, and that
may sound opaque, but it's true and it's raw. We share so much
just based on being human beings, but what I've noticed is that
some people want to feel good about themselves by looking
down on others. It reminds me of a pastor that talked about
people who say they have nothing in common or can't agree,
but he talks about finding common ground and discussing the
ways we relate, in order to be able to discuss our differences
and move forward. I want to be different and better just on the
level of respect and kindness in how I view and treat people
whether I agree or disagree on things. Plus, hey, I don't mind
that he has tattoos. I like them and think that the ones he has
are very nice, colorful, and interesting. They look great.

Adam told me that he was grateful to work with such
a cool girl like me. He always says that it is his job for the
customer to have a wonderful experience that keeps them
coming back.

I wondered if a lot of the time people don't get judged
for having tattoos or for having a lot of them. It depends on
the people, but I have seen that there are still some people out
there who have preconceived notions, and it does hurt other
people when judgments are made against them.

I asked Adam more about why he started getting
tattoos, and he said that he got them because he liked them,
and they meant something valuable to him. He said that
prejudice and judgment don't feel good but that he has a good
support system who doesn't judge him. He went on to say that
some people have even thought something was wrong with
him for being heavily tattooed, but he tries to just prove them
wrong and show them who he is as a person. He also said that
depending on the circles that he is in, no one really cares or

looks at him and that it is becoming more commonplace. He told me that having tattoos has even caused some people to jump to conclusions and assume that he has done or would do certain things simply because he has tattoos.

I have seen firsthand just how kind and caring of a person he really is too, and I know that people have misconceptions about him. I am not advocating for tattoos in the sense of telling people to get them or that they have to like them, but I *am* an advocate for treating people with respect on what they want to do—learning, getting to know them, and seeing past that. We are people.

The next day, Adam invited me to a beach bonfire with him and his girlfriend, Tara. She's eight months younger than Adam. Tara is a corporate lawyer from an affluent family, and she has no tattoos. Adam is totally okay with that and has not pushed her to get any. It has no bearing on the relationship that they have. They are a beautiful couple with lots of love and fun together. People see Tara as squeaky clean. The dynamic is beautiful to me, and they accept each other. When it has come up, Adam has said that he doesn't mind that Tara has no tattoos, nor does he persuade her to get them. He knows that she doesn't want any personally.

Tara said that when they first met more than a year ago, she didn't think much of his tattoos, but as they started to get to know each other on a deeper level, she was somewhat hesitant to take it to the next level. She slightly wondered about what others would think about it, her family, her work, and society. It was different for her, feeling comfortable with it. She fell for the man he was, though, and was deeply drawn to his personality early on. She saw his heart and couldn't shake the feeling that she could not be without someone that great. She is also attracted to him. Most would say that he is very attractive. The butterflies and feelings for him soared and they felt a close connection and bond. Most of the time people don't stare at them when they go out, but sometimes they do, depending on where they go.

She has heard criticisms from people about being with someone like him, but they have both helped each other. Just by being himself, he has helped her to be more open-minded and to think critically outside the box, maybe more with her heart than her head. She has helped him to be the best version of himself and has not judged him. The warmth, trust, and support that she gives him is exactly what he wanted in someone to love. It is what she wanted too. They have fun together and share similar interests, values, and beliefs. Tara now loves Adam's tattoos and thinks that they are cool and nice. She loves them for and on him and finds them to be very appealing. She knows that they partly make him who he is. Her parents accept him, which she appreciates too. They see how he treats her; they know how she feels about him, and they like the man that he is. She is learning to deal with society.

Learning about Adam and being of some help changed my life that day and gave me an experience that I never had before. People take hurt and rejection differently, but at the end of the day we are human, and the truth is it can hurt. Adam is a straight shooter and somewhat direct. Tara said I was a heroine for sticking up for Adam when she heard about it, but I like to think I am just a decent human being. I love talking to him and Tara, who are very nice and easy to talk to. I found the meaning of grace. I felt energized and new from knowing them both.

Chapter 2

It's a beautiful morning, and I am at De La Lina. Mike said that his nephew, Jason, was going to drop by with some things he had to give him. I have never met Jason before. When he walked in, I saw a guy about five foot eight or five foot nine with dark black hair and brown eyes. He's about twenty-four years old. He spoke with a bit of an accent, and at first, I thought it was a British accent, but I quickly began to think otherwise.

"Hey, what's up, Jason?" Adam shouted as he gave him a fist bump. My coworker Lindy came up to me and asked me if he was from England.

"I really don't think so," I said. "I think it's something else. I wondered that at first too, but then I realized it wasn't and maybe it's a lisp or a speech impediment."

"Hey Lila, I have to run some errands to the depot to stock up on some items but Jason is going to help out here because he's worked at a restaurant before and knows what to do," Mike said.

"Okay, no problem." I nodded and went on with my shift.

Working with Jason was nice, and we all decided to catch a movie after our shift that we all wanted to see. It was me, Adam, Tara, Lindy, and Jason. Behind us in line to get snacks was a little girl. She heard Jason asking a question to the movie theater worker and said, "Mommy, what is wrong with that guy? He talks like an alien." The mother looked mortified and tried to shush the girl. She didn't know whether to apologize or act like we didn't hear. I knew that Jason heard though because the look on his face was that of deep embarrassment and sadness. He was quiet. I didn't know if I should say something or leave it be. I thought about whether it would make it worse or not. I always have a curiosity for people and why they do what they do, maybe that is the psychology in me. I am studying it.

Lindy had nothing to say other than an awkward smile, and Tara had a look like she felt so bad for Jason. She expressed that with a look of care that she gave him but from her perspective she later said that she didn't want to add insult to injury by bringing it up and reliving the moment. Jason had his head down and was trying to look away. I could tell that Adam felt bad and compelled to stand up for Jason and address the situation in a nice way. He turned to the little girl's mom and said, "May I?"

"Please, by all means."

"He's not an alien but wouldn't that be cool because aliens are unique and go to outer space, which is a huge achievement," Adam said to the little girl. "Everyone is different, and that's okay too. It's a good thing, 'cause wouldn't the world be boring if we were all the same? We can try to think about how someone might feel."

The little girl apologized to Jason and added that she does think that aliens are cool. She learned that day about understanding. Her mom whispered thank you and gave a bowing smile. Adam smiled, and then we carried on with getting our snacks and going into the movie. Tara took Adam's hand and gave him a look of endearment.

"He's the one who's the hero," I said to Tara.

"You both are," Tara said.

"Adam, I really appreciate you stepping in with that little girl and her comments. You didn't have to do that," Jason said. "Don't mention it man, I got your back," Adam answered.

After the movie ended, we decided to go out to eat. Lindy went home because she was tired, so it was me, Adam, Tara, and Jason. We discussed life, work, our interests, and the things we'd been going through.

Jason shared with us that he has a speech impediment that he has been self-conscious about his whole life. He worries that people won't understand him, and he feels embarrassed about it.

"I understand that," Adam said. "My little cousin has something like that. Sometimes people don't understand people or things that are not like them, and they judge or discriminate. Just be tough skinned because, as hard as it is, it's on them and not on you."

"Thanks, man, I really appreciate that," Jason said. "Do you guys get treated badly or stared at when you go out sometimes?"

Tara replied, "In the beginning Adam would come to my job on my lunch break, and people would make comments that were a bit questionable. They would question why someone like me, a lawyer, would want to be with a tattooed waiter.

"It can be a dog-eat-dog world, but Adam is my prince," Tara said. "He is an incredibly kind human being, who is always fun to be around, and anyone who meets him will realize that it is hard to mistreat him. Sometimes there is a stigma, judgments, questions, and comments, but a lot of the time, no one cares. Others don't blink an eye or comment. They seem to accept it. And then there's the people who say that it is cool or that they like it. Some people ask friendly questions about it, like, where did he get tattoos, and what do they mean."

Adam agreed with her.

"He is brave and strong too, and he has a boldness

about him which I admire," Tara said.

"Do you want any tattoos also?" Jason asked.

"I don't because it's just not for me and not something that I desire on my skin permanently or would be sure about committing to in case I wanted to ever take it off. The process of going about removing it in the event that I change my mind is difficult and painful, but I wholly accept and like it for Adam," Tara said.

Adam is a volunteer firefighter, so when he is doing that there really isn't backlash in that setting. He is also heavily suited up there too, so people don't often see his tattoos. Those that do either have them too, don't mind, or praise him for the work he does anyway.

"And for the other part of what you may have meant," Tara said, "Adam and I don't really face racism, in terms of me being Black and him being White. We have heard some slight comments or questions before that just acknowledge our racial difference but nothing major for us."

Jason said that was good and we went on with our dinner. We had lots of laughs, camaraderie, and fun that night. Before we left, Jason told Tara and Adam that one day he hopes to have a relationship like theirs. He said the way they finish each other's sentences, know what the other is going to say, just by laughing or saying one simple reminder, and the way that they laugh together is so nice to see and inspiring. He said it is like they are the same person.

The next day at De La Lina, Mike told me that Jason told him about what happened at the movie theater and what Adam did for him. He was very grateful. It had been something that had affected Jason for years and really impacted his psyche, so much so that he didn't go to college.

Mike began to tell me more about it. In his school

years, Jason got bullied over how he talked. He began to withdraw and hated school presentations because he worried that people would laugh at him and make fun of him. It got so bad that he would miss school and stay at home and cry. He hated how he was, and Adam had no idea how that simple gesture of stepping up and saying something to the little girl impacted Jason. Adam being brave and saying what he said was timely and right for Jason. Adam set the tone for teaching someone to understand the differences of others and to show respect. I was floored. Someone who has experienced some form of prejudice—although it might seem mild compared to other things—boldly helped someone else who experienced it in a different way and for something that they couldn't help.

"Jason is self-conscious which affects his working, his schooling, and even his friendships," Mike said.

Mike was a strong influence in his life and started to get him out of his shell and into working with him in the restaurant.

"Jason wants to go back to school to do something he loves, and I hope to encourage him to apply to school," Mike said. "I told him that he would find the right group of people who didn't judge him and who uplifted him instead, and to go for it."

After our shift, Adam, Jason, and I went bowling. Adam and I asked Jason what he would want to study in school, and he said that he always loved voice acting and would watch animated movies, practice in his room and dream about how incredible it would be to do voice-overs and act in that way for movies and shows. He always dreamed about it, but it wasn't something that he ever thought he could attain. Adam told him that he should go to acting school or audition and network. He asked us if we thought he could become good at voice acting, and Adam said, "You can be good at anything that you put your mind to and want to do. You can do anything, and yeah, I could see you succeeding and achieving. You can't listen to the critics. There will always be people out there who say you can't do this or that, but you can if you try."

Adam encouraged him to try out and follow his passion. He told him that he knows the feeling of not being accepted and how walking into a room with people staring at you with disdain can feel like daggers.

"But you can take pain, right?" Jason said, jokingly.

Adam laughed. "If it's good pain, that's worth it. It's not so bad. Seeing people stare though and think terrible thoughts about you and your character instead of accepting you for who you are can feel like garbage but what I've learned is that when you can overcome that and be stronger, be better, and be yourself, you can overcome anything and feel like you are on top of the world. Believe in your purpose, believe in yourself, and most of all, believe in God, that he will place you exactly where you are meant to be and show you the beauty that's in the world.

"Tara has helped me to learn and see a lot, she's made me better and strive more and she says that I have taught her a lot too about being open-minded and seeing beyond skin-deep," Adam said.

Jason told Adam that night that he was going to apply to an online acting program and look for auditions to get his foot in the door.

I was so happy for Jason and so happy that Adam was able to make a difference. Mike was thrilled to see the sunshine within Jason and how happy he looked. He got his spark back. I like to think that the sun shined in him too since I had been praying for him. In one of my classes we had been learning about the verse that talks about laying your life down for your friends, and even though it may seem like it was in a small way, Adam helped Jason selflessly with something that could change the trajectory of his life.

I told Jason to not forget me when he becomes famous. We both laughed, and he said he could never. As the days went on, Jason told us that he had two auditions. One went well but in another they berated and belittled him about why he thought he could even do it. They said he wouldn't amount to much and was in the wrong field. They told him that he could only try out for a comedy because his voice was comedy. I saw the brutality in those words when he told us, tearing him to shreds like he was a million little pieces of nothing.

I saw the hurt in Adam's face as Jason told us these words because his heart broke for him. I let Jason know that there would be hurdles but that he would find the right audition company and that it would work out. I told him not to give up and that those people will be sorry when they see his name in lights one day and see him receiving accolades for being one of the best in what he does and leaving that kind of mark. I told him that he could start with making his own videos and skits and get it out there that way. Get yourself up, dust yourself off and get back out again.

"Don't beat yourself up too much. The people who have bullied you are the ones with the issue and it reflects on them not you," Adam told him. Adam and I both knew that Jason struggled with self-esteem and confidence. Even though Adam has dealt with prejudice for his tattoos, he is confident, strong, and doesn't have low self-esteem. I wanted some of that to rub off on Jason. Even though judgments hurt Adam, he isn't ashamed or sorry of the choice he made to get tattoos, and he embraces it. "Ignore the naysayers or speak up when you encounter them," Adam said.

The industry of voice acting can be hard, but Adam and I believed that he could do it. Adam told him that he was going to talk to Tara about whether she knew of anyone who was looking for voice actors because one of her client companies works with that industry. They would tell them about his interest.

We started to wrap up the night. Adam had to teach CrossFit in the morning. He just recently got his certificate to teach CrossFit and was excited to help people in that way as well as with other fitness.

The next day Tara came by De La Lina and told Jason that she had good news.

"So exciting, one of my partner lawyers in entertainment law has a client who is looking for voice actors and wants you to audition," Tara said. Jason was excited yet nervous. We encouraged him to go for it, and he did.

He auditioned and got the part in a children's show as a guest actor. The show would start soon, and we were all ecstatic for him.

We all went out to dinner to celebrate. At dinner we had another interesting experience. We were sitting by the fire pit in the courtyard after we ate, there were some games like cornhole on the grass. Two ladies came up to us. We wondered what they were doing. Then they went up to Adam, and one of them touched his arms. They said they wondered what his tattoos felt like, and then they asked him what his personality was like or what made him want to get those.

Tara, being the protective girlfriend that she is, jumped in before Adam could answer. She said that it's not polite to touch someone without asking and that Adam is a human being, not an object to be touched. She didn't say it in a rude way, but she spoke up. I looked over at Adam and he had a smile on his face. Tara went on to say that while his tattoos have become a part of who he is and how he looks, it doesn't change his personality and character. He is still a regular person who works, eats, sleeps, gets tired, works out, gets hungry, has emotions, and has to do stuff just like everyone else.

The lady who touched him said that she was curious about it because she doesn't meet too many people who have so many tattoos and who look approachable.

"I don't like tattoos," the lady with her said. "It's unnecessary, and I think that it is abhorrent to desecrate your skin and make something so unnatural. Plus, tattoos are bad for you. It can affect an MRI, affect your liver, other medical tests, and it can cause reactions in your skin and system. Plus, it literally damages your skin. I guess you like pain!"

I sat there and wondered what would happen next. Tara was getting ready to speak up when Adam said, "Babe, it's okay." He turned to the lady and said, "Everyone is entitled to their views and opinions on what they feel is right or wrong for them to do. Having tattoos is my choice that I looked into years ago. I got them done at a good, safe, and clean tattoo shop, and I haven't had any negative reactions to it within my skin and will cross that bridge if and when it comes. I tolerated the pain of it, and everyone's level of pain is different. To me it was worth bearing it for the final outcome that I'll always have. You don't have to like the way it looks—that's fine—but it is something that enhanced my skin in my mind, not damaged it. We can agree to disagree and just respect each other's differences. Can you do that?"

The lady looked at him, sarcastically said sorry, and then walked away.

Jason looked over to Adam and asked him if that made him angry or hurt. He said no, he didn't mind explaining it. Adam said that it's not that he needs tattoos or was unhappy before with how he looked but just that he likes them and the meaning of his.

"You are one of the nicest people I know, Adam, and you have helped me more than I can express, so just remember that," Jason said. "Plus, I have heard that it boosts the immune system when it initially tries to fight an infection and can reduce cortisol levels."

Adam nodded his head yes, patted Jason on the back, and said, "Anytime."

Then this group of teenage boys walked in and sat near us. They heard us talking and started laughing at Jason. One said, "Look at this clown, he can't even put words together."

"Why? Just walk away," Adam said.

The boys continued to laugh but walked away. I could see Jason trying to hold back tears as I saw the bullying and verbal abuse that he has experienced was flooding back into his memory and becoming a public reality right now. I told him that we were his tribe and that while it hurts, it doesn't matter what people think. They are the problem, not him. Jason shared with us how frustrating this was for him and that he works with a speech language pathologist. It's a lifelong process for him.

Later that night, Adam told Tara and me that it really messes with his mind how bad some people face discrimination. He said that tattoo discrimination is one thing based on a choice, even though people shouldn't react like that, but that going through other forms that are worse really gets to him. I admire that about him as a person. The next day, we were all happy to hear that Jason was also having success with his voice-acting skits on YouTube. He even got hired locally to do skits for an agency. Getting a chance to do what he loved to do and gaining confidence in the process made me happy.

To be a small part of his story made me feel so good. Helping others, making a difference, and making someone feel good is what I live for. All I can think about is my WWJD bracelet that I have held onto throughout my life.

I won't forget the time when I was little in church and I heard the verse about doing to others as you would have done to you. The golden rule. It stuck with me. It doesn't matter if I agree or disagree with someone, if we are different or not, or if we understand each other on everything or not. What matters is that I treat them how I want to be treated. What matters is that I make a difference and stand in the gap.

At De La Lina, on break, Mike asked if he could talk to Adam and me outside about Jason. We were in the courtyard surrounded by swaying trees, string lights, and a pond. He thanked us for our help and support with his nephew. He also said that he was going to thank Tara when she came by later too. He wanted to tell us that right before we started talking to Jason, hanging out and encouraging him, he was on the verge of giving up and hated himself. He hated his speech impediment, being different, feeling like he never measured up and people making fun of him. Feeling defended, motivated, encouraged, and supported by us, though, changed everything for him, and for that Mike was eternally grateful.

Adam, in his humble and manly ways, bowed his head down with a smile as if to say, no problem at all. I said that I was happy to help, and that Jason is a great guy. Mike said that Jason felt shame but that we brought the best out of him. I told Mike that I know that Jason will continue to thrive and flourish with voice acting and with everything that he sets out to do. We would be there to watch and support. Mike was very appreciative.

Adam nodded in agreement and as we walked back in. His eyes widened and he smiled. "You did it, heroine," he said.

"Adam, it was mostly all you," I said.

"No, never," he said. He smiled and went to get ready to serve a table. He had friendly, kind, and courteous tables as of late, which made us all happy.

I tell myself that although there are bad people in the world and bad things happen, there are shining lights like Adam and Tara. People like them make the world feel like the best place with the kindest people. I always want to believe that there is beauty in every day, in everything, and good when there is bad. I know there is. I look down at my wrist. On one of my bracelets, it reads back to me, *"God is within her, she will not fall."* The Psalms speak to me and sustain me. I know that God is for me, with me, and guiding me no matter how I feel.

🌿 Chapter 3

The next day at De La Lina a pretty girl walked in. She looked about thirty-one years old with silky looking black hair, brown eyes, and a somewhat slim frame. Tara looks like that too, but sometimes her longer, naturally curly hair is straight.

Being the observant person that I am, I watched her go to the bar by the big brown flora pendant lanterns hanging beautifully from the ceiling and order cranberry juice and water. Adam went over and asked if he could get her anything to eat. She politely said that she was good for the moment with food but might get an unsweetened iced tea soon.

Tara came in to De La Lina for dinner and to be around Adam. She sat by the bar as well and wore a pretty dress and her hair in a bun with one piece down in the front. Tara looked over at the girl next to her with her pretty smile and said, "Hi, how are you tonight?"
"I'm doing well. How are you? I'm Monica."

They got to talking, and Tara learned that Monica was a paralegal. They hit it off talking that night and discussed their careers, as Tara is a lawyer. They related on many things and seemed to get along well. They talked about their interests and goals. Tara told Monica that Adam was her boyfriend. Monica told her that she was lucky to have such a good- looking and nice boyfriend. From what I saw and heard, it seemed like she wanted to say more about him, but she hesitated, paused, and withdrew from further comments about Adam.

After our shifts, Tara proposed that we all hang out back at her house in her backyard. It's a pretty backyard with string lights, couches, a fire pit, and a nice ambiance with trees in the background. She also has a pool and a hot tub facing those views. Adam, Monica, and I went over to her house.

We spent the rest of the night laughing, talking, learning more about each other and Monica, and sharing stories on the couch by the pool. The night was still young for us. Our conversations were lighthearted and also deep. It was a great night and we planned to meet again.

The next day I was with Tara and Adam back at Tara's house, and we were sitting at the dining table. Our friendship developed quickly. Tara was telling us about the day at work she had. It was my day off and Adam's day off as well, so he taught CrossFit in the morning and was free the rest of the day but was going to firefight at night.

"Guys, there's a new lawyer named John at my firm, and he's been acting funny around me. He doesn't want to delegate any tasks to me even though we are working on a project together. He doesn't acknowledge me much, and I get the feeling that he doesn't respect me or deem me as capable of being a good lawyer," Tara said.

"In meetings he doesn't make eye contact with me and he even talks down to me and around me. It was becoming a lot so today was the day that I asked him about it. I was polite, professional, and just told him that I feel that he dismisses me. I asked if there was something that was causing that. He told me that he prefers to work with other lawyers at the firm and questioned my law degree and how smart and capable I was. I asked him why he preferred to work with other lawyers, and he said that he is just more comfortable and trusting with other people. He walked away from me and I started walking toward my office," Tara said.

Tara has been working really hard to become partner. She even graduated summa cum laude from school.

She told us that when she was working at her desk, the office secretary who she is really friendly with told her that she had something that she wanted to tell her. The secretary admitted that she debated whether she should tell Tara because she didn't want to hurt her or cause trouble, but she felt obligated to tell her because they are work friends. She enjoys talking to Tara.

Marci, the secretary, was walking down the hall to fill up her cup of tea and overheard John telling another lawyer that he would rather work with his twelve-year-old niece than work with Tara. He went on to say that he doesn't know why they let people "like her" work as a lawyer and that she doesn't look like a lawyer.

Continuing, he said that people like her should not be on the same level as people like them. The other lawyer who he told that to was asking what he thinks she should do instead, and he said, "Maybe be a rapper or something." John laughed, and the other lawyer smirked but then told John that Tara is a good, hardworking lawyer. She has a high success rate and is meticulous. John responded by saying that he was surprised that people like her could be that smart and good. The other lawyer smiled nervously and walked away.

After Marci heard the conversation, she felt terrible because she knows and likes Tara. She also completely disagrees with racism. She said she debated it for a second but then started to walk toward Tara's office. She knocked on the door.

"Tara, can I talk to you for a minute?" Marci asked. She told her what she heard. Emotions of anger, hurt, and sadness filled Tara. She thanked Marci for telling her, and Marci walked away with her head down and an expression of grief. She let Tara know that she was there for her and then let her be alone.

Tara wasn't sure what to do yet, but for the rest of the workday, she avoided John and did her work. She texted Monica a little bit about it, who consoled her and offered her not only support but empathy and an uplifting talk. She could relate in similar ways but with different circumstances. Of course, Tara also texted me and she texted Adam. She asked us to meet her at her house after work, and that's when she told us her story in detail.

After she finished, tears rolled down her face. Adam got out of his seat to sit closer to her and put his arm around her. Her head fell into his chest under his shoulder. He wrapped his arms around her as she cried. I looked at his face and saw emotions of disappointment and hurt. He was visibly upset. He said that he wished that he could have been there for her to take her pain and defend her. He knew he couldn't relate to it personally and that made him unsure of how to comfort her, but he knew that he loved his amazing, beautiful, kind, hardworking, Black girlfriend.

"Tara, I am so sorry that happened," I said. "You don't deserve it." I passed her some tissues and touched her arm. She nodded her head to acknowledge and show gratitude for what I said. Adam told her that he loved her.

The doorbell rang, and I said I would get it. It was Monica. We welcomed her in, and when she heard the story in full, she was upset. She told Tara and I that it is hard being Black and female. It's double jeopardy with many things, and on top of it, being a lawyer as a Black woman is a minority within a minority.

"It's hard, girl," she said. She went on to tell us that as a paralegal she doesn't face as many stereotypes or prejudice as Tara does as a lawyer being on top. But being Black, she gets how it feels with racism and with stereotypes. She encouraged her to talk to her boss about it, and we brainstormed ways to handle her coworker.

"As a Black, female lawyer I feel that I have to work twice as hard as my White male counterparts to be respected and taken seriously. I am the only Black female lawyer at my firm and only one of three Black people working at the firm. I feel shut out, like they don't respect me as much, and now I hear the truth of the matter on how they really feel," Tara said.

She said that she always feels that she has to overcompensate because she feels that people will be surprised that not only is she a college graduate but she is also a JD as a lawyer. She graduated top of her class with the highest honors. Adam told her that she is an amazing lawyer and will continue to excel in her career. We started to talk about other stereotypes that she felt too.

Monica looked over at Adam. "As a White man, I know you can't relate to this," she said. "Feel free to listen or if you want, you can go now so you don't have to be bored or offended with us venting and complaining about White racism."

Adam told her that he loves Tara and anything that affects her affects him.

"I know that as a White man I can't understand firsthand what it feels like to be judged by the color of your skin and to be treated like less than a person because of it, but what I can do is come alongside her and listen, support her, and try to be a change in the world," Adam said.

"I wish I could talk to the guy for you. Seeing you hurt hurts me and is personal to me being that you are my girlfriend."

He also said that discriminating against someone because of the color of their skin, their race, something that they cannot control, didn't choose, and viewing them as inferior because of it is disgusting, ignorant, and something that he will never understand.

Monica asked him if he sees race, and he said that visually he can see it, but it doesn't change anything to him or matter in a negative way. It doesn't define or determine who a person is, he said. Monica said that was good and that it seems like he respects cultures. She said that she had to get going but would call Tara tomorrow. That left me, Adam, and Tara.

Tara laid in Adam's arms.

"I am so sorry that happened. You are the best lawyer I know," Adam told her. I agreed.

I thought about the Bible verses that say not to show favoritism. It reminds me of how they treat her at work, and I reminded her how God created all people in His image. I told Tara those verses, and she agreed and said that she wishes the coworker didn't show favoritism and believed that all were made in God's image.

"Thank you for sharing those verses Lila," Adam said. I admired him for his strength, not just in his words toward Tara but in his actions of how he comforted her and was there for her and how he remained kind even when Monica was slightly rude to him. As a White man, we all knew that Adam couldn't relate to Tara in that way and would never experience what she has, but his support and love means the world to Tara and is so appreciated.

I know there is not an intentionally judgmental or racist bone in Adam's body, and he believes in Tara, and Tara believes in him too. I asked Adam if he felt that the judgments he gets about his tattoos come to mind when he hears about what Tara faced.

"While I do face stereotypes and judgments sometimes, this is different and worse," he said. "I feel for people who have it worse than me and wish that people would just treat others with tact, respect, and stop judging," Adam said.

It hits close to home for him too, being that it is his girlfriend experiencing this, and seeing her upset really upsets him.

The next day at work, Tara decided to work on the project by herself and not really include John in it. She decided not to talk to her boss about what John had said for now and decided to just be a hard and good worker like she always is. She walked in the hallway with boldness as her long, dark hair swayed, wearing a straight down purple skirt, black heels, and a white blouse with a matching purple suit jacket.

John stopped her in the hallway. "Hey Tara, I'm going to start on the deal now," he said.

"I already contacted the partners, so that part is done."

He looked surprised. "Oh, well I guess you are one step ahead."

"John, I'll do my part and you do yours, then we'll give it to the boss."

"Okay." He walked away wondering what the change with her was.

Later that day, at Tara's house, I was there with Adam and Monica. We were talking about how it went with John. "I stayed out of his way. I feel more comfortable that way," Tara said. Monica was a little short with Adam with her expressions and words, but he just remained nice and respectful to her. He kissed Tara on the cheek, said bye to Monica and me, and headed to De La Lina for his shift. I followed behind shortly for my shift too.

When Adam left, Monica started saying more. She told Tara that Adam was very good looking and charming but asked her, "Isn't being with a White man exhausting? How can you feel comfortable talking to him? He doesn't get it. He doesn't get what we go through: the stereotypes, the obstacles we face as successful Black women. He can't really appreciate your Blackness because he doesn't understand or know it. He's not it, and he can't have that perspective. Don't you want a Black king?"

Tara wanted to be defensive when she heard Monica say this and felt insulted but then realized it could be a teaching and learning moment. She paused and said that Adam is the best man that she has met and been with. She loves the way he loves her.

"He is everything that I ever wanted. He is not Black, yes, but why should that matter? He treats me amazingly well, we connect, he is fun and up for anything, he makes me laugh, and he's the most caring and loving man. I feel comfortable with him. He defends those who can't defend themselves, and he treats everyone he meets with dignity and respect. He never crosses lines or says questionable things. He chooses to be understanding. He didn't choose to be White, but he chooses every day to be a decent human being, and he is. Why would I hold his Whiteness against him? It doesn't make him any less or more the man that I want. Sometimes talking about race can be hard or uncomfortable for me, but he tries to create a safe space, and it is something that I am working on, being more vulnerable with him."

Monica nodded her head as if to imply she heard her, but then said, "So when you tell him about the stereotypes you face and racism, isn't it awkward?"

"He's a man that I am in love with, so we talk about things we go through," Tara said. "He is my best friend. He is really supportive and tries to be understanding and open.

He listens."

"Well, I couldn't be my true self with a White man," Monica said. "He is a literal representation of why we are in this struggle and feel that we have to work twice as hard to be respected and still get treated like the underdog and get met with stereotypes."

Tara was about ready to ask Monica to leave her house and was starting to get more offended, but then she thought about how Adam reacts in offensive situations and thought she would follow after him in this particular situation because it was obvious to her that Monica didn't get it.

"Monica, we all have to do what we feel is right. I look past Adam being White, and if I hadn't, I wouldn't be with such an incredible guy. I know who he is and how he is. I don't need to shut him out because of his race. He had no say in his race, but I am physically attracted to him, and that is okay. Race is one aspect, but I can be myself with him. Racism isn't his fault. I love him, Monica."

"Well, I don't know how you do it or look past that. I would think about it every time I see him. White men just can't get it and don't make me feel comfortable after all the history between our two races. I'm not gonna say you're a sellout because you're a Black woman and I know you work hard and are strong, but you crossed lines, I'm just saying. I like you though, and I think you're a rock star." Monica stopped it there and asked Tara if she wanted to go get food.

Tara politely declined and Monica left.

Tara told me about her frustrating conversation with Monica and expressed how she felt. She was wondering how she could handle the situation going forward. I agreed with her that it was frustrating and told her that maybe Monica has that perspective from something in her past. She was offended and hurt by what Monica was saying. She told me that I was such a psychology student in a good way and that I could be on to something.

I told Adam about Monica's feelings, with Tara's permission, and he took it with grace. He said that all he can do is treat Monica with respect and hope that she'll warm up to him.

"It's unfortunate that she feels that way about me," he said, "but things happen in life that may draw that idea, and it's not who I am. To her I represent that just by being White, and I get that. I hope once she gets to know me more, she can be comfortable and see that you don't have to judge a book by its cover and that I am not like that. There's nothing wrong with Tara and I being together and maybe she can see how our relationship works well regardless of race."

I smiled and agreed.

"Thanks Lila," he said. He went on to serve his tables. He had nice customers all day except one cranky table, but it wasn't personal, plus Adam can't control the way that the food comes out. He does his best to serve his tables promptly and communicate with the kitchen staff. One table was just wanting to quickly order and not give him the time of day much. They were usually like that with all the servers, though, as I had seen them before. Adam knew the drill by then and was just the best server that he could be to every table.

"Hey Adam, can you stay longer to help out? A couple people called out," Mike asked.

"No problem Mike," Adam said.

"Thanks Adam, I appreciate being able to count on you."

Adam was always helping out and Mike relied on him a lot because he knew that he could depend on him and trust him. Adam was one of his most responsible employees.

Adam told me that the next night he was taking Tara out to a waterfront dinner. He had a sharp grayish shirt to wear with guava pants, a stylish gray sweater, and dressy gray loafers.

I asked him what the occasion was, and he said that it was just because. I smiled and said "Aw, that is the sweetest. Tara will love it."

"Adam, if you have a minute, I want to ask you for some advice," Mike said.

"Sure, what's up?" Adam asked.

Mike told him that Jason had some new, questionable friends who he was hanging out with sometimes, but they constantly laughed at him when he struggled to say words, and they imitated him and made fun of him. He thinks that they are friends because they let him hang out with them.

"I told him that if he feels like they are making fun of him, then they are not his real friends," Mike said.

"Jason wondered what you thought too," Mike said.

"If they imitate and make fun of him, then they are not his friends. It sounds like they are using him to make a joke out of him for their own false pleasure and gain. It is harsh, not mature and those are not real friends or people that he should be around. He should stick around those who treat him well and treat him like the human being that he is instead of using his impediment to make a joke," Adam said.

"Thank you for saying that. That's how I feel too. I wanted another sounding board. I will let him know," Mike said.

Mike also told him that he was one of his best workers and that he didn't know what he would do without his efforts and hard work.

"You go above and beyond, Adam," Mike said.

Adam thanked him for saying that and for being a great manager too. When Adam turned around, he saw Monica behind him.

Monica said that she heard what he had said, and it was very good. She told him that she caught a glimpse of why Tara likes him and sees how they are a good match. He smiled and asked her how he could help her. She said that she was there for takeout. He took her order and offered her water or iced tea while she waited. It wasn't very busy at the time, so she started a conversation with him.

"I don't mean to be rude or state the obvious, but you have a lot of tattoos from your neck down, did that hurt?" she asked. "Do you regret them? Do you want Tara to have them too? It had to have cost a lot. I know I ask a lot of questions."

Adam had to gather his thoughts for a second because he wasn't expecting to talk about his tattoos right then. He wasn't offended, but he just didn't expect the barrage of sudden questions.

"It has a feeling to it," he said. "Yeah, it hurts and can be tough to sit through for hours; that's the hard part, but I can handle it. It was worth it for me to get the designs. I don't regret getting them, and I have a high pain tolerance, I guess. I am happy with them. It costs money, but I worked hard to afford it and managed my money well, and no, Tara getting tattoos or not is totally her decision. I care about her either way. It doesn't affect our relationship, and I wouldn't push her to get them. We've talked about if she ever wanted any or would get them, and I know that it's not her thing. I respect what she wants, and she respects that I do have them. She doesn't try to change me either, and she accepts me for me as I do her. There's more to our relationship than tattoos."

"Well, they are permanent anyway, and cheers to all

of that. I like your tattoos as you do too since you have them," Monica said. They made small talk. She thanked Adam for serving her, tipped him, and left.

The next day, Adam picked up Tara to go out to the dinner he had planned for them. He pulled up in his Mercedes Benz G–Class SUV looking sharp, and Tara looked beautiful. He opened the car door for her, and they went out to an overlook on the mountains after dinner. Adam parked the car and opened the back. He took out a blanket for them to sit on and a picnic bag with delicious snacks, fruit, water, and some sparkling cider for them to enjoy that they both really liked. They sat and talked.

Adam asked Tara something about work, and she told him she was working on some interesting cases and that it was an interesting day. They had a new intern who asked her to make copies. She had to tell them that she was a lawyer there, and they felt bad after. She told him that some days she feels that she has to prove herself.

"Adam, you know I listen to diverse music, but when it happens to be hip hop, I turn it down when I arrive at work because I don't want people to think, *Of course, the Black girl is listening to rap music, what else would she like?* And with rock I turn that down because it might be unexpected that I like it or that I shouldn't especially if people don't know the history of music."

"Babe," he said, "you can't worry about what ignorant people think. It'll drive you crazy. You can also like any genre that you want."

"Sometimes it's hard. I know on the surface I seem like a strong, hard-core attorney, and I am, but also inside of me, I feel the feeling of being the only Black woman in the room. You are never really the only White man in the room at places. I feel that I overcompensate for stereotypes that people may think of me even outside of work, like that I am not educated, but the reality is that I have a college degree and a law degree.

"Another stereotype that I combat is having a father. I have a loving, caring, strong father who has been married to my loving, caring, strong mother for a long time. I grew up in a family like that. Sometimes people initially assume that it wasn't the case. If someone says that I talk like I am educated, or 'White,' as some people call it, it's just silly and ignorant when you think about it. That narrative has to change. It's just proper. Others say that I sound Black too. There are always little comments at work that make me feel inferior, but I enjoy being a lawyer. I know I am articulate and well-spoken with reading and writing. These are things that surprise some people or that they don't expect, and it causes me to overcompensate," Tara said.

"Babe I'm sorry that you feel that way and face that. I didn't know that you felt that way to that level."

"Yes, when meeting someone, I always wonder if they are going to be surprised when they learn more about me—or even if they will think that I cry racism all the time or that it's not real. But it is—or at least worrying that people stereotype or judge me is real, even when blatant racism isn't present. Microaggressions or the stain of racism, the remnants of it, are present."

Adam asked Tara what he could do to help. She told him that he could just keep being himself—not only with her but with other people he meets—and continue having friends that are minorities, because surrounding yourself with other people can open your mind and help you to be aware of what other people are like, or differences, which can prevent ignorance.

Adam told Tara that he was grateful for her opening up to him and trusting him with this because he knows that it is a hard topic and that the history of racism in this country is something that has frays that linger from it.

"Is there someone at work that you can talk to when John and others make you feel uncomfortable?" Adam asked.

She responded by saying that with the exception of two other male, Black lawyers, everyone at her firm was White and mostly male, although there were some other women. She said that she didn't want to bother them with it.

"I am here to support you, and we can figure this out together," Adam said.

She told Adam that he always stands up for the underdog and offers them a different perspective, and that is what he can continue to do.

"I admire you and I am so happy for the person you are." Tara told him.

Adam kissed Tara's forehead. "I love you Tara Bear," he said.

It's a cute nickname that he has for her sometimes.

"Don't let them make you feel like less than a person. You're not," Adam said. "You are the brightest light, the brightest person, the best lawyer. I admire your drive, dedication, your light, your passion, and I know that the best is yet to come. I believe in you Tara. Continue to be proud of being you, babe, completely you, and when they judge, it's on them. Stereotypes suck and can make you feel less than, but you are not less than, believe that. I am so blessed and honored that you want to be with me and that I'm with you because you are amazing, kind, and beautiful."

Tara lifted her hand to the side of his face, gave him a

kiss, and said thank you. His words melted her heart, and the way that he believed in her made her feel unstoppable. It was an enchanting night, and they enjoyed the rest of it together, caught up in beautiful conversation of the ebb and flow of life and magical ambiance, scenery, and the treasure that they found in each other.

The next day we were back at De La Lina, and then later that night, Adam, Monica, and I were back at Tara's backyard. Tara and Monica both had news to share with us.

Tara said that at work John got reprimanded for failure to perform well, which led them to realize that he was trying to steal money from the firm and do other dishonest things. He then got fired.

"That jerk was doing all of that yet trying to make it sound like you weren't credentialed to be a lawyer and that he couldn't work with you," Monica said. "He stuck his nose up so high, yet he is so low. Good for him, and good for you, Tara."

Adam was happy as well that Tara didn't have to deal with him anymore and so was I. We knew though that she would still deal with stigma and other people that may come along. We all asked Monica what her news was, and she said that she wanted to apologize to Adam for judging him and being short with him and standoffish. It was her past experiences with other White people that made her apprehensive about him, but as she got to know him firsthand and hear what Tara had to say about him, she realized that he is a good person who she can give a chance to.

She opened up and told us about the time that she was called the N-word at a playground when she was a kid. And she shared a story that she once went on a date with a guy who was White, and he made comments about her hair texture, tried to touch her hair, and asked questions that made her feel different. She got a sense that this was how White men were with Black women, but once meeting Adam, she realized that she was passing judgment on him for being White, just like judgment was passed on her for something that she never chose but shouldn't be ashamed of.

Adam told her that it was okay and that he appreciated her apologizing. She went on to share some of her other negative and positive experiences with race. I think we all understood a bit more why she was apprehensive to trust Adam, and I think that she understood a bit more about why she could, or why it was okay to.

After Monica left, it was Adam, Tara, and I. Tara thanked Adam for being a great example of a human being with poise and for being her role model with his compassion, how he deals with people and problems, and his strength in every adversity.

Little did I know that this was just the beginning of seeing Adam's character play out, because the things that would unfold and the people who he would encounter are mind-blowing.

Tara thanked me for being there for her continuously too and for my insight in all things. We had a deep discussion the rest of the night about God and about life. I like to believe that God knows more than we do, as we are finite. He made us, and I know he is beyond us.

Living my life to follow after His guiding moral light and being an example, although I am not perfect, is what I strive to do. Adam and Tara agreed. We discussed going to an upcoming concert event. It was going to be our favorite Christian rappers, singers, worship bands, good uplifting speakers, and pastors, and we knew that it was going to be a great night. We planned to invite Monica and Jason too.

Adam kept in touch with Jason, and he is doing well with his voice acting and with his confidence. Adam gives him a pep talk from time to time when he needs it, and we know that Jason appreciates it. He's gotten in with a good group of friends who all appreciate him for him. Adam is humble, so he won't tell you that it's a big part of the influence he has been on him. He will just tell you that I am the one who saves the day. He really embodies the verse about seeking justice, loving mercy, and walking humbly with God. Sometimes I think that I can't let my lights go down because it helps someone, somewhere in some way.

⚘ Chapter 4

Adam went into the city to drop something off to one of his tattoo artists and to say hello. While he was in the area he got some stuff for the restaurant to help Mike out. He went after his shift at De La Lina. It was night, later, but not too late. It was a busy night for the trains, the buses, cars, and people walking by. Adam walked down the street, hands in pocket, hoodie on, with his charming good looks and natural confidence.

He was passing by an area where not as many people were as he walked back to his car. It was a bit of a long haul from where he found parking to the places he went to, but he didn't mind walking. He didn't get the chance to work out earlier in the day because it was a busy day with work, so he figured walking would be good.

He heard noise coming from an alleyway to his right, not far from the train station. He looked over and saw a group of five guys near a woman. From the distance it looked like they were attacking her. Without hesitation he rushed over and said, "Hey! Get away from her!"

The guys had the lady on the ground with a hammer. She looked disheveled and had some dirt on her skirt, her blouse was ripped, her hands were bloody, and she had scratches on her face. They had their hands on her mouth so that she wouldn't scream. One of them got up and tried to hit Adam, but he blocked the shot and took the guy's arm down. Another came from behind, jumped on his back and tried to punch him in the face by his neck and nose area and kick him, but he threw him to the ground.

Adam used to train at a mixed martial arts gym with

his friend, and he works out every day and teaches CrossFit, so he knows how to handle himself when he has to.

One of them said, "Hey, let's go," and took the lady's wallet. They ran away.

Adam began to take her hand to lift her up from off the ground and make sure she was okay. She sat up. It was dark, and she was dazed and in disbelief that she had just been mugged and attacked.

She looked at Adam and in a faint and shocked voice said, "If you had come a minute later, it would have been much worse. They would have maybe even killed me. You saved my life."

She was fully conscious but couldn't move much. She said that her ribs were sore. Adam called 911. He waited with her for them to come evaluate her and take her in. It helped that he has firefighting training, so he knew what to do, but he didn't have equipment with him.

While they waited, she told Adam that she was scared and shouldn't have been walking by herself like that in a city as a female. She was taking a shortcut from the train but tried to be cognizant of her surroundings. She told him that being a woman can be hard when it comes to safety and that once he showed up, his presence changed everything.

He sympathized and told her that she would be okay. The ambulance and police came for her, and they took a statement from Adam.

When the guys ran away, he had shouted, "Stop them!" to anyone nearby that would hear and act while he tended to the lady. The lady who got attacked asked Adam if he could go to the hospital with her, and he did. He met her there since he had his car and called Tara, Mike, and I to let us know what was going on.

Tara was with her mom and grandma in another nearby town and was going to get there as soon as she could, but I was off from work at De La Lina, so I went to meet him at the hospital.

In the waiting room I told him that I was proud of him and asked him how he did it. He told me that he used to train mixed martial arts with his friend and that when he saw a woman being attacked and whimpering, all he could think to do was stop it. He also said that being a firefighter volunteer helps. I asked him if he was scared, and he told me not really. It happened so fast, so his adrenaline was pumping and it was an intense moment of quick thinking.

The doctor came out to give us an update on the lady. He told us that she had a couple broken ribs, a ruptured spleen, and some bruises and cuts. She also had some defensive wounds. She would recover, but she needed a blood transfusion.

The doctor told us that we could go back and see her if we wanted to. Before we went, he put his hand on Adam's chest and told him that he was a hero and that another minute too late could have been much more serious with the damage that the group of men were inflicting on her. He praised him for what he did.

The doctor told us that we could go into the room. Adam and I went in. Facing us were white walls behind her bed and a cup on the tray next to her bed. Adam was holding his hoodie in his hand. As soon as I saw the lady sitting in the hospital bed, thoughts of disbelief rushed through my mind. Adam's tattoos on his neck, arms, hands, fingers, and legs in his tank top and knee-length shorts were shining as I looked into the lady's face and back at him. I saw the gulp in her throat and her facial expression of surprise and embarrassment. I knew exactly who she was. Adam didn't look fazed. He looked stoic.

"It's you," she said. "Thank you very much for what you did for me tonight, for saving me, talking to the police, and doing the report, for coming to the hospital and for being here right now. I owe you my life."

"I was just doing what anybody would do," Adam said. "You're welcome."

"No, not anybody would intervene in a five-on-one attack on a stranger," she said. "Especially a stranger who has been incredibly nasty to you. I didn't realize it before with everything going on and the shock of it all, plus you had a hoodie on, but now that you are in that tank top, and we're in the light, and I'm in this hospital bed and can see you better, I realize that you are the waiter from De La Lina."

Adam nodded his head yes. "I realized it was you when I started to pick you up from the ground and as we waited for the police to come."

"I'm Madeline."

"I'm Adam, and this is Lila. She works at De La Lina too."

"Yes, I've seen her. Hi Lila, thanks for coming."

I shook my head to say *no problem.*

"Adam, I am very sorry for the way that I treated you. I feel embarrassed now."

"It was those unclean tattooed hands that you took today," he said jokingly.

Madeline smiled and bowed her head for a second. She thought it was funny as she laughed and appreciated that he could have humor and be lighthearted about it, but she also felt terrible for how she treated him and for the things she said that overshadowed it all for her.

"What can I do to repay you?" she asked. "Not only for saving my life but for the terrible way that I treated you."

"Just treat everyone with the dignity and respect that they deserve. Treat them in such a way that they will never feel feelings that you wouldn't want to feel and feelings of judgment," Adam said.

"Why did you feel that way about him when he was your server?" I asked.

"I honestly don't have a good or justifiable reason for it," she said. "He has a lot of tattoos and I wondered what would make someone want to do that and change their body. Someone unhappy with their natural self? It was something different for me, and the stereotypes that came along with them were ones that I actually believed. I thought that if you didn't care about your body so much as to damage it and go through a painful process of needles to change it so much with ink, I figured you didn't care about other things, like health or cleanliness. I thought maybe he did drugs and other bad things and that that was why he had tattoos. I'm ashamed to admit it, but I thought maybe he was dirty."

Adam nodded to acknowledge Madeline but didn't say much. I told her that he was the complete opposite. He doesn't do drugs, he is clean, and he does care about his body. He works out. He cares about what he eats and puts into his body. He teaches fitness classes, and he's a firefighter volunteer. He's a happy person. To him it is just an art form and expression of what he wanted to do on his skin—a story of who he is, what he likes, and he likes the way it looks.

"Certainly, I am seeing a glimpse of the type of person that he is from what he did for me tonight and I regret treating him that badly and thinking those things," she said. "I was wrong."

"Yeah, he is a person with feelings, and judging him that badly really hurt him," I said. "He is one of the kindest, nicest, most loyal, consistent, there-for-you people that I know."

She said that she was very sorry and very grateful.

"Once you realized it was me when you picked me up, you could have left, or you could have told me that you knew who I was, but instead you stayed, you waited for the police, and you are here now. Why did you do it?"

"I am not perfect," Adam said. "When you judged me, it did bother me, just like anyone else, so I don't want it to seem like I'm a saint. I'm not, but in everything I do to help people, and in this case to help someone that treated me the way that you did, I did it because you needed help. You are a person, a woman, and I couldn't just leave you there alone in pain and hurt to get hurt more or to suffer. I just thank God that he gave me the strength to be able to help you."

"I love that. That's amazing to me that you could do that. I didn't deserve it," Madeline said.

"I serve a God who gives much even when we don't deserve it. You know, in church, our pastor was talking about not just going to church but being the church. We *are* the church, and so, in my life, Christ is my foundation on which I have built my life on. So, to be the church to someone, to help them, to love them, to offer peace, hope, and love when I get the opportunity to do that, that's what I want to do. It's who I want to be," Adam said.

"I love that, you learn, listen and carry it out. That's really good. I'm grateful that you were there. Why were you there?" Madeline said.

"Thank you. Lila always talks about her WWJD bracelet, and it's inspired me. I have a necklace of it. The reason I was in the city tonight was to give a drawing of it to my tattoo artist. He wanted to get it for another client, so I gave him the drawing of it that I made so that he could see my idea. I also was picking up things for our manager while I was out.

"Oh wow, that is inspiring," Madeline said.

"Thinking about WWJD motivates me because none of us are like Jesus. We are fallible, but he still sacrificed for us. I can follow in his ways. When someone first invited me to their church and I went, I found hope, purpose, and direction that was beyond me and more than '*I could ask, think, or imagine, according to his power that is working in us,*' like the Bible says. I found life and shared that with my family. The vibe, atmosphere, community, and what I learn there is peace to me. Honestly, I want to be that to someone else just as a person, as a fellow human who cares and wants to exude what I found and how life changing it is—a better way. So, I didn't do it for praise. I did it because you needed help and I couldn't just watch a human being suffer when I knew I could help."

"Wow, that is so inspiring Adam, the way that you exemplify that and carry it out. You know your stuff. You're a good influence even when you've received disrespect. Tell me more," Madeline asked as she sat up in her hospital bed astutely and with a sharp curiosity.

Adam smiled. "For me, living for God means loving others even when it's hard. I make mistakes but God forgives so how can I not forgive others."

I chimed in. "It reminds me of the verse that says, 'Bless those who curse you, pray for those who mistreat you,'" I said.

"Right. I'd rather live for him and be wrong than not live for him and be wrong. I think about what Jesus did for me and for us," Adam said.

"I am really blown away, and to think I placed so

much emphasis on tattoos. This is thought-provoking and profound," Madeline said.

"Tattoos are just my art form. Yes, it's permanent. It doesn't mean I don't love myself. I just like how it adds to me. I like how they look. It expresses me in ways, but it doesn't define my character or my whole person. There's more to me than just my tattoos. At the end of the day, I'm a person who does the same things that you need to do."

"That is powerful, the faith that you have, the way that you exemplify it and the way that you explain and see things," Madeline said. "Thank you for sharing that with me. I wish I hadn't judged a book by its cover. I was very wrong."

Just then the doctor walked in and told Madeline that they were having a hard time finding a blood donor for her blood type. They were still trying but time was of the essence. She needed a blood transfusion.

I offered to pray for her that the doctors would find a match. She said that would be nice and she accepted and appreciated it. Adam and I prayed with her. Adam asked her what her blood type was. She said A negative. Adam said he was A negative blood type too. I was B positive.

The doctor walked back in. "Adam, you are A negative? I was going to ask if either of you would like to donate blood, but I wanted to wait to see if a match came through first."

Adam looked over at Madeline.

"Adam, I hate to ask, but if you could, it could be life or death," Madeline said.

He said of course.

The doctors took him back to prep him and ensure that his blood was a good match. I told him I would call Tara. I did and she arrived at the hospital with her mom soon after.

Her dad was out of town on business. Tara, her mom, and I waited in the lobby together. I told her the story in detail.

"So, Adam saved this lady that was horrible to him at the restaurant, judged him, didn't want him to serve her, said all this stuff about him and he is now donating blood to her?" Tara asked.

"Yep, and he didn't tell me it was her when I first got here before I saw her," I said. "I think he didn't want to upset me because I was there when it happened, and we discussed it and he knew that I felt bad, or maybe he just wanted to be humble."

"Right, or maybe he wanted to forget about it," Tara said.

"He's a good man," said Tara's mom. Adam's mom joined us in the hospital waiting room and hugged each of us as she walked in. She has shoulder-length, brown-blonde hair, bluish-green eyes, and she is very nice. She came in and thanked Tara for calling her so that she could be there for her son and with us. She told us that she was very proud of Adam for the man that he is and that from the time that he was a child, he stood up for others. He would even do it with his play toys.

Tara's mom had to leave at this point because she had to go back to help her mom, Tara's grandmother, with something. She told Adam's mom that she would call her soon to check in. I told Adam's mom, Tammy, short for Tamra, that she raised a really awesome son who is kindhearted. She thanked me and said that she can't take full credit—his dad, her husband, had a lot to do with it too. She joked that Adam gets it from her though. As we waited, we talked about Adam and what he means to us all and shared good conversation and comfort together.

                                M.N. Walters

Time was ticking, and Adam was done giving blood. He came out. We asked him how he felt, and he said he was okay. He looked kind of groggy. Tara and his mom hugged him first and offered him some water.

When he first saw his mom he said, "You came, Mom."

"Of course I came, I'm your mom," she said. "Tara called me. Dad is on the way too, but I'll let him know that you are done."

I asked Adam if he knew how Madeline was doing, and he said the doctors said she would be okay and that she is taking to the blood well so far. She is resting now and said that when she gets better, she wants to treat us to lunch and come by De La Lina another time with him as her server.

"Isn't that ironic that the lady who didn't want you to touch her food or have you serve her because of what's on your skin now has your life-saving blood within her?" Tara said.

"Yeah, she couldn't pass that up," I said. "It literally saved her life."

"I'm not as forgiving with everyone and good as Adam. It can be hard," Tara said.

"It really makes you think and realize as people we are all the same in a way, and everyone should be respected," Adam's mom said. "You never know what could happen or when you will need someone."

Tara said that she would drive Adam home as she didn't want him to drive yet in case he was dizzy. She came with her mom, so she didn't have to worry about leaving her car. We said our goodbyes until the next day and Adam's mom said that she would call later.

I called Monica and let her know what was going on, and she couldn't believe it all. She really admired Adam for his bravery and selflessness. She said that if someone had done to her what Madeline did to him, she probably wouldn't be able to do what he did for her. Monica shared that Madeline shouldn't have been walking alone in a dark alley and that she herself gets scared when walking in a city or waiting in a car alone in certain settings. Guys call out to her or try to approach her, but once her brother or a male friend comes, and they meet, the guys back away and stop. Tara told her that was one unfair thing about being a female and that we had to be extra careful in our surroundings and environments.

The next day Tara was at Adam's house hanging out in sweatpants and a T-shirt. Adam was in the same.

"You look cute, babe," he told her as she walked back to the couch with a cup of iced green tea for him. She was there keeping him company and making sure that he felt okay from the blood transfusion and was having enough liquids.

She sat next to him on the couch. "You amaze me, Adam."

He smiled and ran his fingers through her hair. "I love you, Tara Bear. Thank you for taking care of me."

She made a *you got it* expression, put her dainty feet with her beautifully pedicured orange-red toes on his lap, sat back, and went to put a show or movie on the TV.

He told her that Madeline texted him that she was recovering well and couldn't thank him enough for what he did. He said that she was also apologizing a lot and joking that after all that she did to him, his tattooed blood was now in her blood, and the very thing and person that she despised is a part of her now metaphorically.

Tara smiled. "You are better than me, Adam. I couldn't do it. To treat someone with such openness, kindness, and respect and go above and beyond when they treated me like that. I applaud you for how you handled everything with her. I can't think of being with a better man than you."

They hugged and he told her that she has been good like that in situations with how she carries herself.

Later that night they texted me to get together the next day. We have become close friends since that night at De La Lina that really brought us close together.

The next day we were at De La Lina, and Tara stopped by. She asked us if we wanted to go on a trip to Salt Lake City, Utah, in a couple weeks. There was a concert she wanted to attend for an up-and-coming new rock band.

Adam told her that he wanted to go too and would talk to Mike about his schedule.

I said the same. It sounded fun going away with Adam, Tara, and one of their other friends. We all love music and singing. Adam also plays guitar, drums, trumpet, and a little piano. In high school, he was in a band with some friends.

When the trip came and we got to Salt Lake City, we got our Jeep Rubicon rental car and explored the city. We took pictures, screaming as our hair flew wildly out the sunroof as Adam drove. His close friend, Branson, sat in the passenger's seat.

We were touring the city: trying food, hiking, biking, dirt biking, sightseeing, shopping, going downtown, and going to a motocross event. We stopped at places we saw that looked nice and interesting.

The concert came on our second to last night in town and we were all excited for it. We got ready and arrived at the concert. We pulled up at the arena and took our seats. The band was slightly delayed starting, so we were waiting. The group of three guys behind us were obnoxious. They were loud, inappropriate, spilling their slushies, and kicking the back of our chairs. They were crass. In our row was Branson, Adam, Tara, me, and some other people.

Tara turned to me and said, "This guy keeps putting his feet up and kicking my chair." It went on for a little while until she finally turned around and politely said to him, "Can you please stop kicking my chair?"

He ignored her at first, kept doing it, and then spilled some of his slushy on her back, which dripped down her shirt. She turned to me and said, "What's his problem?" She then looked behind her again and said, "Hey!"

The guy stood up boldly and said, "Clean it up!"

"Excuse me!?" Tara said.

The guy responded by looking at both Tara and me and said, "Go home, you don't belong here. We don't want you here!"

Tara stood up and asked him to repeat himself.

Two of the guys stood up, and one said, "We don't want your kind here, Ms. Dark Skin. Shouldn't you be at a rap or R&B concert?"

Adam stood up. "You need to stop now. Watch yourself. You don't talk to her like that."

One of them looked at him. "Or what? What are you guys doing with them anyway?" he said to Adam and Branson.

Tara spoke up first. "You racist—"

"Babe!" Adam said. He didn't want things to escalate with the disrespect directed toward Tara and me.

"Babe?" the guy said. "You are a couple? Wow, can't imagine what that's like. That is disgusting to even think about. I couldn't stomach it. Hope you overpower her and make her serve your every want and need like she should!"

"Back down!" Adam said firmly and angrily. "What's disgusting is how you're acting." He turned back around, tapped Branson's chest to say let's go, grabbed Tara's hand, and said, "Let's go," with protection and authority. "Lila, let's go," he said to me firmly. "We don't need to listen to this."

Branson followed behind. The guys were still making comments, and as Branson walked past them, he said in a somewhat quiet voice, "You guys really need to stop. They don't deserve to be treated like that."

As we walked to the car, Adam said that the guys were ignorant beyond belief and not worth it.

Branson was at a loss for words by the whole thing, and I could tell by the expression on his face that he couldn't believe what was going on and felt embarrassed—not because of us or by us but because we were experiencing racism right before his eyes by fellow White people. He hadn't been in a situation like that before. Honestly, none of us had been to that extent, and we had been to plenty of concerts.

We walked to the car. Tara was livid and sad, Adam looked angry and disturbed, and I was processing everything and trying to tell Tara that it would be okay.

The guys followed us to the car and were yelling racial slurs as we walked. "Should we write the N-word on the window?" They trailed closer behind us shouting.

Adam told Tara and I to get in the car and lock the door. The guys were really close to the car now, and Adam turned around and said, "What's your problem!?"

"Those two are our problem. They don't belong here, and since you are on their side and with them, neither do you!"

Adam shook his head. He turned to Branson and said, "It's not worth our time. We don't belong here because we don't belong in ignorant spaces."

"Do you want a piece of me?" one of the guys asked.

"No, I'm not going to stoop to your level. Back down," Adam said.

"You know one of them is a lawyer," Branson said.

"Oh, I'm scared," the guy said.

Adam and Branson got in the car, and Adam started driving away. The guys chased the car for a minute on foot and then stopped. We reported it. Adam also planned to call the next day to get us a refund, and I thought, *We may have missed the concert that night, and maybe we could have moved seats, but honestly, Tara and I didn't want to stay anymore anyway.* I ended up getting a text alert that due to technical difficulties it had to be rescheduled anyway and that refunds would be issued.

The car ride back to the rental where we were staying was quiet. Tara was staring out the window on the passenger's side, Branson was in the back seat on his phone, I was observing everyone from the back seat, and Adam was driving but looked really upset.

He told us that he was so sorry that we had to hear and go through all of that and that he couldn't believe those guys. He said that he felt embarrassed that it happened. He asked us how we were feeling.

Tara didn't say a word.

I told him that it was very offensive, hard, and that what I thought would be a fun night was spoiled by those people and brought down the vibe and positive atmosphere. I told him that I couldn't believe that it had happened. It was offensive and scary. Tara and I are both minorities with two guys who are the majority as White men, and in that moment embodied White privilege and power at its finest, but these guys are friends and to Tara, one is her boyfriend. Their outside may be that, but who they are as people is what we had to remember. Because, in that regard, we were all in this together even though they couldn't feel what we felt with this personal attack or didn't share our skin color. They were there, disturbed by it, and affected by it, because we are all connected and because it is wrong. They are not racist. I admired how they both stood up for us.

As someone who is Black, with Bahamian roots and also half-Samoan, it was personal for me. It was also deeply personal for Tara, who is Black. Her cultural background is Jamaican. We are both proud to be who we are.

The commotion of the night was unsettling for all of us. Adam and Branson tried to be there and stand by us. All they could use was empathy, but somehow that had to be enough, and it was.

When we got back to the place we were staying at, Adam asked Tara to stay in the car so they could talk. He knew his girlfriend, and her silence in the car was saddening to him because he knew that she was in emotional pain.

Branson said he would go inside and give them some time. Before he went in though he looked at Tara and said, "I'm so sorry, Tara. You didn't deserve that. Anything you need, I'm here."

She nodded her head.

I said that I would go inside too. Branson looked at me too and told me he was sorry that I had to experience what happened tonight. We went inside and talked about what happened. I learned how sweet, cool, and amazing Branson is. He listened and he tried to understand. He made everything feel better. When Tara and Adam came back inside later, she told me that back in the car Adam looked over at her, but she was speechless.

"Tara, do you want to talk about it?" Adam asked.

She was silent.

"Babe?" he said.

She just stared out the window.

"Do you want to go inside?" he asked her.

She shook her head no.

He said, "Okay, we will wait here then. Take as long as you need. I'm here for you."

She tried to fight back tears in front of him. She put her head in her hands and cried. She leaned against the window. Adam wrapped his arm around her, took her into his chest, and embraced her.

"I got you," he said. He felt her shaking, tears running down her face, and she was very upset. At that moment, he was filled with defeat. It was mixed with anger from the fact that he had to watch his girlfriend go through racism and hurt yet again, and that there was nothing he could do to take that pain and experience away—nor experience it himself and understand firsthand what that feels like. Adam also felt sad and hurt. He wanted to make a difference and let her know that he saw her, heard her, and would stand with her.

After a while, I went outside to see if Tara was okay. We were bonded not just as friends but as having a shared experience of being Black women in the face of racism. I asked Adam if I could talk to her, and he said yes. He went inside.

Tara and I had a long talk.

"Dude, that was unreal," Branson said.

"Crazy. It really tears me up to see Tara and Lila affected and go through that," Adam said.

"Man, I feel bad. It's unnerving, and there's got to be something that can be done," Branson said.

"Yeah, I know," Adam replied.

"Adam, man, do you think this is similar in a way to the tattoo issues that we've had?"

"I think it's worse," Adam said. "By far. Racism is a deeply rooted, heavy, lingering issue—much more serious than someone being judged or discriminated against for having tattoos. I've had tattoos for a while now, as you have, and it's just a part of my everyday life, as it is yours. Our friends with and without tattoos accept us, and many people do. It's just you get those who don't sometimes. Sometimes I don't even think about it, and depending on what is said, it doesn't hurt me when people don't like them. It just gets me when it affects my work life or when they judge me as a person over it, like when Madeline didn't want me to serve her and said all that stuff, or if they judge my character and make assumptions. It's just like, why do you feel that is okay or right, you know? I'm pleased with my tattoos, same with you. Since I have a bunch of tattoos, people are naturally curious, and I just embrace it."

"I agree man, it's the same way for me," Branson said.

"It has some comparisons, in a way, but what Tara and Lila are going through is different. I know that we can't relate to it or understand what it feels like, being White men, but I try to be there for them and let them know that I'm here," Adam said.

"Bro, that's what we can do and stand up for them," Branson said. "Letting them know that we support them and care and are in their corner is what we can do. I can't imagine going through it though, bro, and I applaud you for it all 'cause I'm sure that being an interracial couple can sometimes come with its challenges—even just with this situation, responding in the right way. Tara and Lila are the best. This is just mind-blowing."

"I love my girlfriend," Adam said. "She's an absolute boss. She's beautiful, smart, funny, sweet, caring, driven, and she's everything that I've always wanted. I'm proud of who she is. She embodies her middle name, Joy."

Just then Tara and I came back inside. Tara went to her room to change from her leggings and long shirt into some comfy sweatpants and a hoodie. I went into the room with Adam and Branson, and they asked me how Tara and I were doing. I told them that we had a good, long conversation. Tara came out of the room with her long hair swaying and told us she was going to bed.

Adam asked her if she wanted to talk.

She said not yet but that they could talk the next day. She needed some time to gather and process her thoughts. She also said that she wanted to go home the next day and was just over the trip and wanted to get back.

I knew that even though we had had a good time the day before, what happened traumatized Tara, and her anxiety was in high gear. It was a lot and hard to handle. We all agreed to switch our flights so that we could get back to California. I spent the night talking to Adam and Branson about race and racism.

When the next day came, we made our way back home.

Branson asked me for my number. We really enjoyed talking and hanging out.

Tara had texted her parents and brother about what happened. They are all really close, supportive, caring, and loving. They love keeping in touch.

When we got back, we said our goodbyes. Tara and Adam drove together, and Branson picked me up, so I drove back with him.

When Adam and Tara got into their car, Adam said, "I want to take you somewhere." They hadn't talked much since the incident happened.

Tara asked him where he wanted to take her.

"To one of the most beautiful places on Earth. You'll see."

Adam and Tara drove to Big Sur on the Pacific Coast Highway, also known as Route 1, and when she saw it, she couldn't help but smile.

He looked over at her and had this handsome smile and expression when he saw that she was happy. It lit him up. He put his hand on her hand. He drove to the beach, opened her car door, and walked with her to a rock that they sat on.

"Tara, do you know why I wanted to take you here?" he asked.

"Because it was where we went when you told me you loved me for the first time?"

"It's more than that," he said. "It was here that I realized that I loved you. Before I told you I loved you, I remember how it made me feel when I knew that I loved you. Moments and places in life are things you never forget. You know, the day that I met you when you walked into De La Lina, I thought you were the prettiest girl in the room. You were that day, and every day, you are so beautiful.

"Once I started serving you, and we got to talking, I thought that if I could have a shot with that girl, I would be the luckiest guy in the world. Being with you has been nothing short of a blessing. As I got to know you when you kept coming in, and we would talk, when I asked you for your number, and when we went out and then first started dating, I admired you. I admire your dedication, hard work, spunk, love, kindness, drive, and everything about who you are.

"This journey with you has surpassed my wildest imaginations. We've been through a lot together, and I am so proud to be yours and that you choose me every day, Tara Bear.

I want you to know that you mean a lot to me. You are my world. You are beautiful inside and out. Don't ever let anyone steal your shine. No one can ever take that away from you."

"I am enamored, go on," Tara said with a smile as she held his hands and looked into his eyes.

"You have so many assets. You're a successful lawyer who's an absolute boss. You're an incredible person. You are smart, you are beautiful, funny, caring, and driven. You are everything that I've always wanted. You embody your middle name. It's what you bring me, Joy. I am so proud of who you are.

"I remember when I told Branson that about you. He told me that he sees that and is so happy that I found you."

Tara stood there blushing and filled with awe.

"Thank you, Adam. I feel the same way about you. I never knew that this was where you realized you loved me. It's breathtaking here. Thank you for bringing me here. It reminds me of why I love you too and everything that you've meant and been to me. You are hot, you're amazing, and everything that a girl could want and dream about."

Adam leaned in and embraced her.

She looked into his eyes. "I'm sorry about yesterday," she said. "I couldn't find the words to face you. I felt a rush of emotions: humiliated, scared, hurt, devalued. Welcome to my life. I know we can talk about anything, but it's hard at times opening up to my White boyfriend about race, even though I know you are here for me."

"I feel terrible that you had to go through that," he said. "It's not something that you should be embarrassed about. It's not your fault in any way. I'm sorry that you are going through this," Adam said.

"I know it's hard," Tara said. "Are you sure you want

to keep dating a Black girl?"

"This would never make me not want to date you, Tara. You are the best thing that ever happened to me. I'll go through this with you if you let me. I want to take your burdens, understand, and support you. I know that as a White man, I have never experienced racism, and I'm not going to pretend to know how it feels, but I am here for you and can use empathy. I will always fight for you.

"Look at the waves, Tara. Each of them flows and are beautiful. They make a pattern of waves that crash on the shore, perfectly in sequence and constantly, but each wave has a specific wavelength. Different but the same, and that's a good thing. It doesn't make any of them any less beautiful. Some waves are rough, some are calm, and some are higher than others. It doesn't stop me from going to the beach. We adjust accordingly with swimming, surfing, or sitting out. We go to the beach and to the pool. We like both. Every relationship has challenges, Tara, and for us, we get along really well. We get through challenges, and together we can handle racism. It doesn't make our love any less beautiful. In fact, it is so beautiful."

"I love that, you are right and you are so right for me. I am in awe," Tara said.

"You are exactly the girl for me. With the connection that we have, I am forever grateful that we connected, and me being White and you being Black doesn't change anything between us for me. I love you, Tara Joy," Adam said.

"I love you too, Adam James. You know how to make a girl feel better. You make everything better. I remember the day that I started to fall for you. I felt like I was living a teenage dream. The butterflies, the emotions, I couldn't get you out of my mind. And for me too, being with you, the man that you are, you are everything that I want. Not to mention that you are smoking hot," Tara giggled.

Adam gave that charming, handsome grin and said, "Let's go," and they ran into the ocean. They laughed the afternoon away and were playful. Tara felt much better. Adam assured her that he was there for her.

She told him that she filed a report for what happened. Adam supported her in full. They splashed waves in the ocean, and Adam told her to always believe in herself, that she deserves it, and that she has to believe in everything she does: with work, with who she is, with being proud of being Black, with her goals, and with her dreams.

Encouraging her to hype herself up, they started cheering. "It's gonna be awesome!"

I loved hearing about this. It melted my heart.

Chapter 5

After a nice walk and bike ride with Tara through the redwood forests and then to the coastline, I started to get ready for a barbecue at Mike's house. He wanted to treat his staff as a thank you for our hard work and dedication. It was fun, and it was going to be our last hurrah until we got back from our trip to Anaheim.

Adam, Tara, and I are going to Anaheim. It all worked out because Adam is going to a CrossFit convention. He has some clients that he works with, and it is his goal to open his own CrossFit gym. Tara is going for a law conference, and I'm going with them to visit Disneyland and to visit my grandparents who live near there. We are really close.

It all happened to fall on the same week, so we are driving there together. After day one of the conventions, we had dinner together and decided to go out to a baseball game we heard was happening that night. The game was fun, and afterwards we were getting concessions and getting ready to head back to the car. We heard shouting, so we turned around, and behind us was an altercation ensuing between two men with other people gathered around.

One man said to the other, "You freaking m—— is anything inside of that stupid brain?"

The man shouted back, "Screw you, you jerk! You're not going anywhere."

The shorter man then pushed the taller one, and the taller man threw a punch and hit him, which made the man fall to the ground.

Adam went over, stood in between them, and said, "Hey, break it up!"

The taller man said, "Who the heck are you?"

"Look, man, just leave him alone," Adam said.

The man looked him up and down. "Who are you, punk? His bro? Stay out of it."

"Let's just go our separate ways," Adam said.

The man told Adam that he would beat him with his boys, and Adam said, "I bet you will. Just walk away."

The man walked away, muttering, "The m—— isn't worth my time anyway."

"Do you know how hurtful and offensive that word is?" Adam asked. "Why do you have to call him that? He's a person. He deserves better than that."

The man dismissed us with his hand gesture, hissed through his teeth, and walked away.

The shorter man dusted himself off and said, "You didn't have to do that. I can handle myself, but thank you."

"It's not that I thought you couldn't, I just wanted to help," Adam said.

"Help? You don't even know me. I respect that. I'm Sean." He reached his hand out to shake Adam's hand.

"Adam."

Tara and I walked over, and I said, "Hi, I'm Lila, and this is Tara." Tara waved. I asked Sean what had happened. He said that he was waiting in line at the concessions stand and the man cut in front of him and said that he couldn't see him when he said, "Excuse me, I was waiting."

The man told him, "You can wait, you imbecile," and he said he cut back in front of the man, whose wife said, "Stop messing with us, you freak."

He said, "Shut up you fake wannabe trash," and then the man called him the M-word and said, "Don't talk to my wife like that, you freaking troll."

Sean said that he got mad and said, "Screw you both," and then the man kept saying he was going to beat him.

I told Sean that people like that are not worth his time and energy and that the man wasn't right for starting a problem with him by purposely cutting him in line, not trying to wait, and then treating him like he was less then by using derogatory slurs and by his actions.

Sean told us that this was typical life for him, as he has dwarfism. He said it comes with limitations in life as well as ignorance from other people but that he tries to do his best. Sometimes he gets hot tempered.

"Look, man, I just want to say thank you for what you did for me back there," Sean said to Adam.

"Don't mention it," Adam said.

I told Sean that we have all faced hard days and gone through stuff, even if those things are different for differ-ent people.

"You guys seem like cool, great people. Are you from here?" Sean asked.

I told him that we were from Central California by Big Sur, and he told us that he was from Fresno. He was in town for a work conference. He works in sales.

He went on to tell us that there is a lot of bad in the world and that people suck but meeting us and having us go out of our way to help him and stand here and talk to him really made his day and showed him that maybe there is some good left in the world.

I invited him out with us to explore the city and go to Disneyland. He accepted the invitation.

The next day, we were all having a blast at Disney-land. We were laughing, talking, joking around, and being silly. When it came to a ride, Sean was told that he didn't meet the height requirements. We all told him that we could skip that ride and find something else to go on, but he insisted that we did not need to do that and should enjoy ourselves. Adam and Tara went on the ride, but I stayed behind with Sean. Adam can be a thrill seeker and he likes rides. Tara can get a bit scared, but she does it anyway and has fun. I don't like big rides, just small ones, so I stayed behind with Sean.

We had a really good heart-to-heart. He learned about me, and I learned about his job, his family, his travels, interests, and the way his life has been. He told me that in his thirty-seven years as a little person he has seen and heard a lot. Being denied going on rides is just the beginning. When he is out in public, he faces a lot of slurs and people making fun of him, laughing, taunting him, and calling him names. He has met people who don't think he is capable and who treat him inhumanely, he told me. Feeling like the odd man out is something both familiar to him and painful.

He was the first little person that I knew personally. I felt that I was learning a lot from him by seeing the world through his perspective. The jeering that he faced had an effect on his psyche and his view of the world.

He told me that when Adam intervened in the fight, it was new to him because he never had a stranger do that for him. He questioned his motives at first but then started to realize that maybe he really was just a genuine person, so he gave him and us a chance, and so far, we haven't made him regret it. He said that the invite today really meant the world to him. He explained that it is hard for him to open up to people because of the way that he gets treated, so he has a small circle of friends, some little people, some not, but when it comes to meeting new people, it can be challenging for him.

Just then, Adam and Tara met back up with us.

"What are you guys talking about?" Tara asked.

I explained it to her, and she said, "Yeah, we all have our stuff. It is hard that you have to face all of that. For me, it is dealing with racism. I have faced discrimination at work and feel that I have to work twice as hard and be put together a certain way to even have a chance in the room, but this one here has taught me how to actually be the room. Adam and Lila have both shown me how to lead the room. I've gained confidence, and I know my self-worth, but it is hard sometimes, leading rooms full of White men and some women who don't always think you are capable, worthy, or as respected."

"Tell me more," Sean said.

"I also have challenges with my hair. It is difficult to get it straight. I love my long and full hair though. Sometimes I have it curly or thick, and it can be hard to manage. When I go to certain hairdressers, they complain and are rude, especially a certain one, or they ask me certain 'ethnic assumption questions' or comment on my hair. It makes me feel different, and what they say blatantly is asked because they do see me and my hair differently. I finally found someone that is good and not like that. She likes my hair, its beauty and fullness, and we get along well. She never complains about my hair, and she does a good job. It's quick and easy going to her."

Sean was listening, interested, and empathetic. "As a White male that faces a different set of challenges, I hear you, and I would never not respect you in the room," Sean said.

"Even Adam has faced some situations of judgment and assumptions based on having so many tattoos," Tara said.

"Oh really? I think the tattoos are rad," Sean said. "It's in and they look good on you. I am thinking of getting one, I love them. It's nice ink."

"Thank you, yes, there have been a few incidents, but

overall, a lot of people are cool about it. Some ask questions, some judge, but overall, many accept it and like it, and others don't mention it or seem to mind."

"Adam, you *have* faced discrimination over it and judgments. Yeah, it's not every day, and many people do love them and think it is cool or commonplace, but you've had a few scenarios where there was judgment and assumptions over something you like that is an artistic expression of yourself. It's a choice, yes, but it's wrong for people to judge," Tara said.

I added that Adam was humble and doesn't like to make his stuff seem bad because he knows that people have it worse. He thinks it pales in comparison.

"Yeah, I mean, sometimes people will say to me, 'You probably have a gnarly, crazy life story.' They'll ask if I've been to jail, and I always say, I've made some mistakes in life, little things learned, but I've mostly stayed on the straight and narrow. Nothing crazy, never been to jail, there's things that I wouldn't do, so it's like, sorry for disappointing you with a not-so-gnarly, crazy story in that way, but I think I have some good things that can be gnarly too, a positive story in its own right.

"I've had tattoos for a while now, it's just a part of everyday life for me and means something to me. It didn't change me, my work ethic, who I am as a person in character, that's all the same. It doesn't hinder me. It wouldn't," Adam said.

Sean said that he completely agreed. He told Adam that people probably think at first that he is hardcore, but once you get to know him, you can see that he has a big heart and is soft and tenderhearted. Such a down-to-earth guy. He asked Tara if she had any.

She said that she did not but that she really likes Adam's. It adds to his manly, somewhat rugged appearance but with a sensitive and good spirit.

"I think they are pulchritudinous and nice on him," Tara said. "It's a good look."

"That's awesome, no idea what that word means but it sounds good. They do look great," Sean said. "Look it up," Tara said with a smile. "I will," said Sean. "So, going back to what you said before, facing so many racial challenges and dating a White man must come with its set of challenges too?" asked Sean.

"Not as much, believe it or not. He is really understanding, encouraging, and supportive. He listens, he's patient with me, he helps, and I can really be myself with him," Tara said.

Looking at the two of them, Sean said, "That's very sweet. How about for you, Adam? Are the challenges hard to deal with?"

"I love her, and any challenge we face, we can handle and overcome," Adam said. "We take it day by day, and it's not that hard. The hardest part of it for me is knowing that it affects her and that it's directed at her and hurtful. That's what gets to me—not me being a part of it but me seeing racism, prejudice, and discrimination directed at her."

"Oh man, that's got to be difficult," Sean said. "I imagine that interracial relationships take love, patience, respect, and an open mind, so I am sure that you are both that way."

"Yeah, when we first started dating, someone who I thought was a friend at the time started acting differently around me and started saying some really hurtful and offensive things," Adam said. "At first it was behind my back and then they were asking me if I really was serious about getting involved with a Black girl and that it would be different. Then it became like a joke to them."

"Wow," Sean said. "Sometimes it's hard to know who to trust, and really discerning things in life and protecting your peace, mental health, and health is imperative. This is really interesting, listening to your stories. I'm learning from this and really identifying with it in a way. I am glad that you shared that."

I have faced some similar challenges to Tara. That's one reason we bond and how I can help her and walk with her through some of those things. Outside of that, we also just enjoy each other's company. I shared with the group my experiences of growing up in two cultures, how my parents taught us about both and my experiences with racism. I shared my plans and goals of my career as well.

I told the group that this table that we were sitting at was so sublime because here we are: four people with different life experiences, two different races represented at the table. All of us have faced different things, yet we also are cool people who bond and connect over life experiences, some shared, some different, but we all understand the human experience. We are blessed and have a lot to be grateful for. We are going through this journey called life, and not doing it alone.

It makes me think about how some people may say that they don't have anything in common with someone to want to have a relationship with them or care, but to me it's not always about having everything in common. It's about connecting, sharing, respecting each other, and being able to converse and listen to the interests of others without judging them. Acceptance is so easy yet can be so hard for some. I feel that if you can talk to someone, care, and enjoy their company at places that you both like, then that can already build something good sometimes. Everyone agreed.

Sean said that it was true and insightful to put it that

way and to think about it. Sean told Adam that his faith neck tattoo and arm and hand tattoos were inspiring to him.

Adam was grateful and it started a good and deep conversation about the meaning of faith and the meaning behind his other tattoos of strength, beauty, time, family, and life.

Sean expressed how grateful he was to meet us and emphasized that he has experienced bullying throughout his life and feeling inadequate and different, but that it's people like us who make him feel tall. He told us to never change.

We spent the rest of the day enjoying Disneyland and saying how we wanted to go to a waterpark soon too. I told them that I also love Disney World too and that Orlando and Palm Beach County, Florida, are my happy places among other places in the Sunshine State. I love Florida in general. They said that they do too and that we should plan a trip there. There's so much to do. It's pretty, nice, fun, and has great weather and just a great atmosphere and vibe.

When our day came to an end, Sean reiterated that we all must keep in touch and that the three of us immensely impacted his life more than we know. He said that just being there for him changed the trajectory of his life from us being there at the game to spending time talking and getting to know each other. We gave him a new perspective and showed him genuine care. That meant the world to him. Talking to him like a person, inviting him to spend the day with us, sharing our own stories, and listening to his made him feel a way that he hadn't in a while, simply like a person.

He told us that people take pictures of him in public, making things like going to the grocery store hard, and he often feels like he is on display. Meeting us made him feel alive again.

It made me think of Proverbs that talk about words

and wisdom. I hoped I beheld that. Sean told us that he doesn't mind when people respectfully ask him questions about his life related to having dwarfism, but he wants to be treated like a man, not someone that is made fun of for his height and not being able to reach certain things. He is thankful that we did that for him.

Our time together was not unmet with some stares and some snarky remarks by strangers about his height, like, "Oh, can he reach the counter?" or saying, "Look, it's a m——," but there were also people that didn't blink an eye. Having this experience with Sean helped me to learn and see a new perspective. I am so grateful to have learned how someone else lives and to be able to help him see a positive perspective on other people as well as add to his feelings of self-worth.

At the end of the day, he is just a man, and I'm not sure why others don't see that or can't treat him like one and give him the time of day to get to know him. Looking at him, talking to him, respecting him, and getting to know him are things that he deserves despite differences.

It was soon time for us all to head home. Sean went back to Fresno, and we returned to the Big Sur area, but soon we might be off to a new adventure. Adam and I are thinking of traveling to help open a new location of De La Lina on the East Coast, and Tara can work from home sometimes, so she would come too for a couple of weeks.

Sean told us that he would visit us in Monterey and that we were always welcome in Fresno. I told him that we would love to do that, and he was excited to try De La Lina one day. He thanked us again, and we parted ways.

✵Chapter 6

When we got back home, Adam and Tara went out to a romantic dinner after work. They went to a beautiful restaurant with candlelight and roses in the middle of the table. The lighting in the room was perfectly dimmed. Tara told me about it.

Adam had on a nice sweater, stylish black pants, and nice brown boots. Tara wore a pretty flower-pattern dress with an elegant sweater and white short heels. They were enjoying their meal and their evening together. Adam slicked his hair back.

"How are your parents, Tara Bear?" he asked her.

"They are good. My mom is busy with teaching. You know she was a nursing manager at a hospital and doctor's office before that, but now she is a full-time nursing professor. She is enjoying it. My dad is good too. He is busy with his actuary career and just got promoted from vice president to COO and is also doing his real estate investment work too."

"That's really awesome. I am happy for both of them," Adam said.

"That reminds me. I was going to tell you that they are going to have a party next week to celebrate my dad's promotion. Can you make it?"

"Of course, baby."

"Great, you can meet my extended family that will be coming—the ones who you haven't met yet. Some other people will be there: friends of my parents and people that you already know too. Invite your parents!

"I know that Jenny is in South Dakota, so she probably won't be able to make it. Marcus will be in town for it too."

"I talked to Marcus earlier actually."

"Oh, good, I'm glad you talked to my little brother," Tara said.

"He's doing great with his audio engineering career in LA."

"Yeah, he is doing well. I'm proud of him. I love hearing how it's going. How is Jenny?"

"She's good, busy with Dale and her jewelry business," Adam said.

Jenny is Adam's older sister.

"So, how are your parents doing?" Tara asked.

"They are good. My dad is busy working as a project manager, and Mom is busy with her home décor business. She's been designing new home items."

"That's good! I talk to your mom sometimes," Tara said.

"I know she adores you. They both do," Adam said.

Adam smiled and reached over to touch her hands. "How did work go today?" he asked.

"It was good," Tara said. "Working on some interesting cases and gaining more respect. For those who don't respect me, I just try to prove them wrong and try to let it not bother me. I'm liking work. How's it going for you?"

"It's good. Nice customers lately. Some stuffy and demanding ones at times, but that comes with the territory of the industry."

"No one is bothering you about your tattoos though, right?" Tara asked.

"Not as of late. It's great working for someone who accepts and appreciates you for who you are, as Mike does, and many customers have been cool too. But you know, when I go up to a new table, it's like some think, *Who is this tattooed guy*

serving me? But then they realize, *Oh, he's nice.* I get the stares
and whispers, especially at certain places, as you know, and
questions from time to time, but it comes with the territory of
being tattooed.

"I get the *Those are so cool, who did it, and where* questions
too. It hasn't been happening often lately with people judging,
and it is really accepted by a lot of people, but you know there
are those people who have their preconceived notions about
me and who they think I am. Many people in general judge by
appearance."

"Right, I know those stereotypes, and you are only
the good ones, not the bad ones," Tara said. "You are loyal,
committed—I mean, you committed to something permanent
for life, so I hope you are committed in other areas, which you
are."

"Yeah, to me, my biggest thing, my philosophy in life
and how I was raised, is to treat others the way that I want
to be treated," Adam said. "I know how judgment feels, and I
don't want to give that to anyone else. That's my responsibility:
to do better. Being there, being a good friend, son, boyfriend,
and person are my priorities."

"Absolutely," Tara said.

"My mom was like, 'I have to call Tammy and Chuck
and invite them to the party,'" Tara said.

"She loves your mom and dad."

"I know. My parents love them too," Adam said.

"I'm glad our parents get along so well," Tara said.

"So, Tara, I want to give you something." Adam took
out a jewelry box and handed it to Tara.

She gasped with excitement and asked him what it
was for.

"Open it," he said with a smile.

She opened a box with a beautiful necklace with charms on it like an angel, a bear, and an elephant. "Thank you, Adam!" she said. "It's beautiful."

"I got it for you because you're my Tara Bear. I want angels to protect you wherever you go, and let that be a reminder to you, and the elephant was just cool. They are big and smart and I know you are smart and will do big things in life."

"You are so sweet Adam. I love you."

"I love you too," he said.

"How's your food babe? Is the fish good?" He asked.

"It's good, how's yours?"

"It's good. It's a really good restaurant," Adam said.

"But not as good as your food," she said with a smile.

"I'll cook for you soon again babe."

"So, Lila and her parents and brother are coming to the party too," Tara said.

"Okay, awesome. Love Lila," Adam said.

"I know," Tara said. "She's so nice, so caring, and always there for us and up for adventures. She's a good friend to us both."

Adam agreed.

"I'm looking forward to the party. So have you heard from Madeline?" Tara asked.

"Not since last week," Adam said. "Last week she was doing well in her recovery. She's walking fine without any support, feeling better, back to work, all of that. She's progressing well."

"That was a big thing you did, not only saving her but inserting yourself into a dangerous situation and then on top of that giving her blood, essentially saving her life. At first when Lila told me I couldn't believe it, and I felt sort of perturbed, to be honest, that you did all of that for her. Like, I get saving her, and I am glad that you did that, but staying with her and meeting her at the hospital, and then giving your blood. I only felt that because of how she treated you. I felt like my baby didn't deserve that treatment at all.

"It broke my heart when Lila told me about that night, Adam, with her and with the lady with the groceries. I never told you that in that way, but later that night it made me cry. I called Lila and she talked me through it. She really helped me and comforted me. I've learned a lot from her.

"I am all for helping people, and I love that quality about you. It just hurt me to know how you felt. To have someone treat you that way all because of what? Your tattoos and who you are, things you've been through, things that have meaning, and simply because you like them and have art on your skin permanently? To publicly and loudly say they don't want you as their server, and then to call you names and say you are a degenerate, untrustworthy, risk taker, unhealthy, unhygienic, unclean, irresponsible, and to ask you to wash the filth off of your hands? Then to have the audacity to say that you do drugs? Just to make all of those assumptions about you based on that.

"They didn't see you as a person—a human being first and a good server who does a good job. I am thankful for Mike, who supports you and doesn't ever judge you or ask you to change, but I just have to say, it did bother me a bit because I felt that lady didn't deserve what you did for her. But then it reminded me about not only why I love you but about the type of person you are and why.

"I am the most blessed girl in the world to have someone like you. Not only are you extremely good looking, but you have the biggest heart. Your strength and resilience move me Adam, and your ability to turn the other cheek when I'm not sure I could, but I will try to exemplify your love and compassion, just who you are. I want to work on having that more and getting there in my faith journey. Not only do we have fun and are you funny but your character and who you are as a man is unreal to me.

"I know Madeline is sorry now and realizes that she judged a book by its cover, and it wasn't true. Just because you sat through the needles of the ink to get tattoos, which, yeah, it damages the skin and hurts and then heals, it doesn't make you unhygienic. You picked a good artist, you care about showering and being clean, you care about clean eating. You're not in any way a degenerate. You are none of those things, and I trust you in full. Just how could someone say that? Your choice doesn't give them the right.

"I'll hold your hands. I want to make you feel worthy and loved in those moments when the world judges, makes assumptions, and discriminates against you. Some people with tattoos may be those things, but not because they have tattoos, just 'cause that's how they are. Others are not. You have been there for me, and I just wanted you to know how I felt about that night that I never told you."

"Oh wow, baby, it's okay. At first, I was angry and in disbelief, but I realized it was her own problem. I know who I am, and if I let it all get to me every time, I would go crazy, so I try not to. I don't mind people asking me about it in a polite way, of course, but sometimes people take it too far or say rude things. I just try to make it lighthearted with how I respond when they touch me. It happens. Tattoos don't feel any different than regular skin anyway. I just feel bad for people who have it worse than me. Maybe I am a bit of a risk taker—some studies say that—but not too much. I take good and practical risks," Adam said.

"You do. I've known it all my life, and I know you say I've inspired you, but you've helped me to see how to be more like Jesus and treat others that way. You help me to want to do the same. It rubbed off on me. If you can do it when people treat you like that, I can do it too, but it can be hard.

"You have met them with such grace, and anyone who has judged you should feel bad when they see how you treat them," Tara said, looking in Adam's eyes. "Grace and sometimes humor are things you exude, you never meet them with retaliation even if you feel a certain way about it," Tara said.

"Thanks Baby. Yeah, I was at work, and I'm going to be professional at work," Adam admitted.

"But even outside of work you are like that," she said knowingly.

"I try not to get too worked up, but I say something. I'm not silent about it."

"I know, babe, you do, just not in a mean, jerk, rude way, 'cause it's not who you are. You stand up for me, and I love that about you. You lead with compassion and love, and I see it in your actions. In Utah, when you took charge and told us to go in the car and lock the door, when you stood up, I loved that about you. I admire it. Very manly."

Adam put his hands on Tara's and smiled at her and said, "No one messes with my girlfriend. Racial slurs and racism are things you should never have to hear, and feeling insignificant is not something anyone should ever make you feel. I hate that you had to hear that. It was enough, and racism is alive in the hearts and minds of some people, unfortunately. I'm going to stand up to it and against it because it's not right. People need to open their minds and hearts and be understanding."

"I appreciate everything you said, babe. It means a lot

to me. It makes me feel good," she said.

"I feel so grateful to have met you and to be with you, Tara. I also am always excited about you. Being with you is an honor."

Tara smiled and looked into his eyes, which melt her every time and give her butterflies. They enjoyed their dinner together, and the bill came. Adam paid it and they left. He opened the car door for her and asked her if she wanted to come by his house to watch a movie or sit outside by the fire pit.

As they started driving away from the restaurant, Adam got a call. It was from Madeline.

"That's ironic," Tara said.

Adam answered the call.

"Hey, Adam, it's Madeline. How are you?"

"Hey Madeline, I'm good. How are you?"

"I'm good. Did I catch you at an okay time?"

"Yeah, I just finished dinner with Tara, and we are in the car. She's right here."

"Oh, hi Tara!"

"Hi Madeline! How are you?"

"I'm good, thank you. I just wanted to let you know that I am doing well, and the police caught my attackers."

"Oh wow," Tara and Adam exclaimed.

"Yes, I had to go in and ID them. It was a random mugging and incident. I learned my lesson to not walk alone in the dark or in certain areas. So, my case is progressing now."

"Good, I am glad to hear that they were found and that the charges are underway," Adam said.

"Me too, it's looking like aggravated assault and battery."

"Good, it's a relief to hear that things are looking up for you, Madeline, and that you are feeling well," Adam said.

"I really can't thank you enough for all you did for me

even when I really didn't deserve it. After all the assumptions and judgments I made about you, you saved my life. I was so wrong and don't believe any of that anymore. You have the right to express your art, and I know you are clean. Your blood saved my life. Thank you so much, Adam."

"You're welcome!" he said.

"Can I take you guys out to dinner sometime as a thank you?"

Adam looked over at Tara and said, "Yeah, we'll let you know when it will be good."

"Okay. Thank you and have a good night, guys!"

"You too," they both said.

Tara looked over at Adam. "That's good that things are working out for her," she said.

He nodded his head in agreement and reached over to hold her hand. They drove to his place hand in hand.

Tara told Adam that he makes her feel like she's living out her teenage dreams of getting the amazing guy.

He smiled. "I'm not perfect, babe. We all have shortcomings," he said.

"You are perfect for me," she told him. They got back to his place and sat by the fire. They talked the night away.

Branson wasn't home. Branson, who came with us to Salt Lake City, just recently moved in with Adam in his house. Branson's old lease ended, and he figured it would be nice to have a roommate, especially with a good friend. They've known each other since they were preteens.

I saw Adam at De La Lina the next day, and we joked around and laughed. We had good customers—a couple of rude and impatient ones, but that's a day in the life. We talked to Mike about how Jason was doing, and we were happy to hear that he is thriving. Adam said he touches base with him from time to time.

I told Adam that Monica was doing well too and that I was going to see her soon. I asked him if he heard from Sean, and he said that he hadn't but would text him soon to check in and say what's up. We also talked about how we were looking forward to Tara's dad's promotion party. Adam was telling me that he had some gift ideas of what he wanted to bring: flowers for her mom and then something for her dad. He thought about cufflinks and a watch, and I told him that was a great idea and that her dad, Charles, would really like it. Adam loves watches and wears a nice one himself. After our shift we said our goodbyes, and Adam said he would catch me tomorrow at Tara's parents' house. Before we left, as he was walking away, he turned back around and said, "Lila."

I said, "Yeah?"

"Thank you for everything you've done for me and for Tara. I know you've been there for her, and you've been there for me too through ups and downs. You're a really good friend. Through you with the WWJD stuff that you live out, you've taught me a lot."

"Thanks Adam. You've both taught me a lot too."

He smiled. "Catch ya tomorrow!"

"Okay, see you tomorrow," I said. When I got home, I spent the night texting with Branson.

The next day we arrived at Tara's parents' house. Cars, some extravagant, were parked outside the long driveway. As I pulled up, Adam and Tara had just arrived too, and his parents were on their way. My family was going to stop by a little later. We were mingling and talking to people. There were a lot of people at the house. I would guess that there were anywhere from eighty to one hundred people.

Adam, Tara, and I were talking to Tara's parents. Her

dad was saying that she was his precious baby, his princess. Her mom looked stunning in her glimmering blue beaded dress as she greeted us.

Adam handed her dad, Charles, his gift, and he thanked him. He placed it on the table of gifts and asked to talk to Adam privately. They stepped away but still close enough for me to hear what they were saying.

I talked with Tara and her mom. Her mom is very nice, welcoming, and friendly. Her dad is too.

"Adam, you know, I never got the chance to say thank you for what you did for my Tara in Utah. You are a really standup guy, and you take care of my little girl. I'm protective of her, and at first I had my guard up with you because that's how dads are with a guy interested in his little girl. At first I thought, *Who is this guy with the tattoos?* But as soon as I got to know you, I knew I couldn't ask for a better guy for Tara. She really respects you and likes you.

I know in the beginning I was maybe a little cold or standoffish to you for different reasons, but I'm sorry for that. I see how she feels about you, and of course she talks to her mother about how she feels about you. We know how you treat her. I just want you to know that Denise and I really like you and appreciate you," Charles said.

"Thank you Sir. You weren't cold or standoffish to me."

"Okay, good. I'm glad you didn't think so. Enjoy the party. Let me go greet some of the guests."

Then Adam's parents, Tammy, and Chuck, showed up and hugged their son. Tara went over and hugged them both, and Tammy told her that she had something for her that she saw at the store and thought it would be perfect for her. Denise hugged Tammy and Chuck and welcomed them. The two dads got to talking about golf, but only briefly because Charles had to make his rounds with the guests.

Tara and Tammy have a special bond, and Tammy raved to Denise about how great her daughter was, how they raised such a wonderful young woman, and how she has been so good for Adam, brought out the best in him, and really encourages him to be his best self in his endeavors. She told her that she truly made Adam better. Denise was grateful and returned the sentiments about how wonderful Adam was to Tara and to their family.

Tammy went over to Tara, smiling at her. She really treats her like a daughter. Tammy asked her how work was going and if her son was treating her well. She told her that her son is amazing.

"He is a good one," Tammy said. "I am blessed."

I talked to Tammy a lot. Chuck was off mingling with other guests, but he's really nice too.

We were all called together for a toast. Denise got up and gave a speech about how proud of Charles she was from starting his career in his business realms to becoming an actuary, to moving up, becoming VP, to now becoming COO. They talked about when they were young and had their dreams and how blessed and thankful they were for everyone at the party and for their family. It was a great story and a great party. We all enjoyed our time there.

After the party, we went back to Tara's backyard and Branson came out too. Adam was telling us that they had been playing guitar and drums lately again. He said he wanted to join the church greeting team to welcome people when they come in through the doors and help them get connected to different church small groups, Bible studies, and activities if they wanted to, or join the church worship team.

I was happy that Adam wanted to get involved in that way, and I knew he would be good at it because he is friendly, welcoming, and has a way with words and talking to people that is smooth and reassuring. If he went the guitar or drums route, I thought that would be awesome too.

Tara was excited for him too, and she was thinking about helping out with the kids' program at church. I also help out with the greeters, so it was awesome that Adam might be on our team. Everyone there is really great and welcoming, and the faith I see inspires me, making me want more of my own.

As we were sitting by the fire pit talking, Tara got a call from Monica. She told her that she would put it on speaker and that we were all there. We said hi to her, and she was telling us that she's been encountering racism that is really upsetting her. Judgments and assumptions based on her being Black are not uncommon, but this personal issue related to her hair really bothers her, and she figures that Tara and I can relate and help her.

Monica explained that a few years ago she stopped chemically relaxing her hair and thus it is natural now. Her naturally thick, afro-like curls have come back, making her hair hard to do and hard to straighten herself, which is the primary way that she likes to wear her hair. She resorted at first to ponytails where her hair was falling out of the ponytail and bunched up big around the sides. She gets it straightened sometimes, but the job is not done very well when she does it herself and at some hairdressers. She has also encountered ridicule and complaints from certain hairdressers who want to charge much more for her slightly longer than shoulder length and natural hair. They tell her one price on the phone, but then, in person, it is not only a different price that day after the session but for the following session too.

She feels that this is their job, and the complaining stems from both racism and laziness. When she has a difficult task at her job, she doesn't complain or ask for more compensation. She gets it done.

Not only is it a culture bias and lazy, but it is downright rude to tell someone to come with their hair combed next time since it was slightly tangled and that due to having natural hair it will cost more and more and more. Monica wanted a change, so she got it straightened at another hairdresser that she found who used a manageability treatment. Due to the product treatment given and the time and precision with heat that the hairdresser put in, her hair became long and very head straight. The compliments and comments at work were flying.

"You look different!"

"You look extraordinary and extravagant!"

"I almost didn't recognize you!"

"You look pretty!"

"You look beautiful!"

"That's a big change!"

"Is it real?"

"You look skinnier and slimmer!"

This was what she kept on hearing over and over again. The worst was: "You look nice, usually I am used to seeing your hair bushy and big." As if that is bad and not beautiful. And goodness forbid she come with bushy hair another day. Hearing that you look pretty is a nice feeling and compliment but hearing that you are pretty solely based on your hair is insulting. Especially hair that is only temporarily like that based on an expensive treatment and hair salon, or the heat of a blow dryer and a flat iron by a hairdresser who took the hair piece by piece to get it like that. For the hairdresser it's easy.

For me to do it is not.

"So, when my hair is natural, I am not pretty?" Monica asked. "Do I look different? I am beside myself. What should I do? Cut my hair off? I'm sorry that my hair doesn't fit the standard of beauty naturally or live up to other people's expectations. When I had a perm, it was easier, and I guess more beautiful to a very judgmental outside world. It was a lot cheaper too for that reason, and maybe some prices went up also. This is healthier, and we should all have a choice that's met with respect.

"So, when I look 'bad' again, they won't say it, but they'll be thinking it. This isn't my new style, as some say. Who says it will last exactly like this for long? They have no idea how hard it is. They don't understand our hair texture. I love it straight, and it looks good, but the point is, am I worthy when it isn't? Does it define my whole being and outward look? They have no idea what it is like to be a Black female. We face assumptions, stereotypes, hair issues, and we have a history of being treated less than, but also rising in the face of adversity, we work hard, and yeah, maybe that one is a positive stereotype, but I'm fed up.

"With all of that being said, the last treatment was good and lasts, but I decided to just go with a short hair style and cut it, not because of the world but because it is easier for me. I'm liking my new hair style and it fits me."

Tara sighed and told her that she feels her pain.

Adam jumped in and said her hair looks nice in all of her different hairstyles and that he doesn't think one is better than the other.

I told her that I understood her and that all we can do now is let people know how we feel so that they can reflect and process the meaning of their words and the weight they carry.

It *is* personal. It is a direct comment and insult to our race and our ego because, while it is real hair that we have, straight hair for us is not natural hair. It was made like that by heat and technique. Once we wash it, it will get big again unless we get it professionally done again and done well or make our best efforts to do it ourselves with our many products and tools.

"Right, so I am just insulted, and my hair is misunderstood," Monica said. "Compliments are nice, but it is really an insight to how they really feel and really see me, and I just feel this feeling of: *Okay, when it doesn't always look like this, when I don't make it to the salon, then what?* It seems as if I have to answer to these judgments."

Tara told her that she understood and that it really is frustrating. Tara has her hair straight and long, and while the texture is slightly different from Monica's and mine, she stopped relaxing her hair too. She gets it and empathizes with Monica.

Monica was very thankful for the time taken to talk and for us all listening to her vent. "The things you hear being with a Black woman and company, right Adam?" Monica said. "I bet there are things you never thought of or heard before that now you're exposed to all the time. You see the struggles, hair, and just in general."

Adam smiled. "The best I can do is open my eyes and mind and try to understand. Everyone is different but being with Tara has taught me a lot about the struggles, the resilience, and the power. For that I am so grateful, and I have the utmost respect.

"I see what she goes through on a daily basis, having to do with race, and it's tough, but I also see her strength. I'll never fully understand it or know what it feels like to be Black because I am not Black. I don't walk in those shoes, but I can do my best to imagine and be there."

"That is very nice, Adam," Monica said. "You're a really good guy, not bad for a White guy. Tara, girl, you have to keep this one, you have a good one. I learned that. I had to open my eyes too, and I saw who you are, Adam, and you know what? I'm glad I did. It was hard to trust you, being White and all, but you've proven time and time again who you are. Thank you, guys. Lila, Tara, Adam, Branson, thanks for the venting session. I feel better, and I'm going to go get some stuff done, so enjoy your night. Let me let you go."

"Okay, girl, thank you too," Tara said. "I needed that too."

Tara and I have solidified a friendship with Monica. Tomorrow we are getting together.

After the phone call, Tara was going to go inside to get more iced tea. I said I would go with her, and there was something that I wanted to tell her. When we got inside, I told her that Branson and I had been texting and talking and that I really like him.

She gasped with excitement and said that we could be dating best friends. She asked me if he asked me out yet, and I told her that he hadn't yet but that I hoped he would soon. Tara was excited for me and told me that Branson is a really good guy who's been a good friend to both Adam and to her as well when they met. She said that she hopes that it works out for us and that it would be great.

Ironically, when we got back outside to Branson and Adam, I could tell that they had been talking about something similar. Later that night, Branson asked me if I wanted to go out on a date with him that weekend and I accepted. Adam was happy and said that Branson was an awesome guy and that he was really happy that we connected with each other.

The next day, Tara, Monica, and I met up at the park to work out. It was a beautiful day with sunshine glimmering over the palm trees and ocean. It felt great. The plan for the day was to work out together and then they were going to go on a double date with Adam and Monica's new boyfriend, Derek. This would be the first time that the four of them really hung out and got together. I wasn't going because I already had things planned with my parents and brother. Tara said she would fill me in.

Tara had seen Derek in passing before to say hello, but this would be the first double date. Things had been going well between Monica and Derek. Before dinner and after working out, the girls went to a boutique in the mall. Monica wanted to buy something nice. They walked around the store and Monica looked over to Tara. "Is it just me or has that lady been eyeing us?"

Tara looked over. "I think she is," Tara said.

The lady started to follow them around the store. Monica became agitated. She looked over at Tara. "This is nice, do you like this item?" she asked, holding it in her hand.

Tara told her that she did.

The lady came over to the girls. "Oh, that piece is $500," the sales lady said. "We really don't like customers browsing and touching our stuff when they aren't going to buy anything. There is a nice store for window shopping or for cheaper items down the hallway though that might be better for you."

"Excuse me!" Monica said. She couldn't believe what she was hearing but yet she could. She started to fill up with emotion. She knew exactly what was going on.

"Dear, are you in the wrong store?" the woman blatantly asked.

"Are you saying that we can't afford anything here or that you don't want us to?" Monica asked.

"I am saying that this is a store for a certain clientele, and I think that your type of store would be better found elsewhere."

Monica had a shocked look on her face that this was real life and was really happening to them. "You are going to have to help me right now, because I can't," Monica turned to Tara and said, "I don't have the patience or the fortitude for this."

"Ma'am," Tara said, "what makes you think that we can't afford the items in this store? Do you know us?"

"You girls just don't look like my usual clientele. We keep a certain image in this store, and I want to maintain that for the satisfaction of all of my guests."

"What kind of clientele?"

"Ladies, I am going to have to ask you to leave at this point. I need to help other customers and don't have time to watch you."

"Watch us?" Monica said. "Watch us for what? We are fine!"

"I need to make sure that all items are accounted for."

"So, you are saying that we are thieves now?" Monica asked.

"Your kind has been known to steal. I can refuse business to anyone whom I choose if I think that they can't afford it."

Tara shot back. "Well, I'll have you know that she's a paralegal, and I am an attorney. I can afford anything in this store and then some. We both can, but maybe we don't want your overpriced stuff anyway. What you are doing is racist, and it's blatant discrimination. You are following us around the store and saying that we will steal because we are Black. You don't even know us. We have every right to be in here if we choose to be," Tara said with poise and firmness.

"Okay, I am going to call security since you both refuse to leave."

"And tell them we were shopping? What if we wanted to buy something? You wouldn't let us?" Monica asked.

"We don't need your business," the lady said with a scoff.

"We have plenty of Whi— I mean the right customers who can afford it legitimately."

"I am going to report you. This is enough," Tara said. "We will do more than that. We will sue and tell everyone to never shop here again. We'll make it known so that you lose a lot of business. You deserve it," Monica said.

"I'm calling security," the lady said.

"Let them come," Monica said. "Let the manager come too."

"The manager is out today," the lady said, "but you can call another day."

"Monica, let's just go," Tara said. "She's not worth it, and neither is this store."

Monica and Tara left hastily and were rightfully upset about their encounter.

"I cannot believe that happened," Tara said.

"I have shopped there before, and that never happened," Monica said. "I've also never seen her before. I can believe it though. White people are like that.

"I was at a condo once visiting my coworker's grandma, who she wanted me to meet, and the doorman thought I was the driver and the help of her grandma, all because she is White and I am not. I was beside myself. I explained to him who I was. Clearly, he thought I was the help and couldn't afford to live at the place or be someone else, but the way he made me feel and what he said to me, it was degrading.

"Tara, being Black and female is a constant balance of proving yourself and being fully immersed in both identities at all times," Monica said. It's tiring. It's probably why I have a grudge and mistrust against some White people."

"I have an idea," Tara said.

"What?"

"I'm going to call Adam and have him come here, go in the store, and see how he gets treated, which is probably very different than how we got treated. Then I'll go in so the lady can see we are dating. That will set her off. Record the whole thing, Monica."

"Okay, girl, I like that idea. Call him. Your White boyfriend can come in handy now. White privilege at its finest."

"Okay, I'm dialing now," Tara said. "Hey babe, are you busy right now?" She asked him.

"Hi baby, no, I just got off work, and I was gonna go work out before I pick you up for dinner. It's at 7:15 with Monica and Derek, right?"

"Yeah, it is. I am with Monica right now at the mall, and we are dealing with a racist lady in a store. I'll explain later, but we need you to come and walk around the store to see how she treats you. Monica will record, and after a little while, I will join you in the store."

"Okay, I'm like ten minutes from the mall. I'll swing by there now."

"Thanks, baby! You're the best. Drive safe."

When Adam got to the mall, the ladies briefed him on what happened, and he walked into the store.

The lady saw him and went up to him. "Hello, sir, how are you today?"

"I'm good, thank you, how are you?"

"Good sir, let me tell you about our promotions today, and let me know if I can be of any assistance to you at all. The men's section is over there, and I am sure that there are some lovely pieces that you would enjoy that would look great on you!"

"Thank you," he said.

"No problem. I'll be over there if you need me." The lady then went away to help other White customers too. She didn't follow or stare at Adam at all.

Minutes went by. Then Tara reentered the store. The lady looked at her with disdain and started to follow her. Tara went near Adam but didn't say anything to him just yet. He looked over at Tara and she gave him the cue. Adam looked over to the lady with a smile, and she rejoined him.

"Is that girl over there disrupting your shopping experience?" she asked.

"Not at all. Why would she be?" Adam asked.

"Oh, I just want you to have a good shopping experience, and you know they are different from us. They are not like us."

"What do you mean?" Adam asked.

"She probably can't afford anything in this store even though she claimed to be a lawyer before. Even if she was one, it's just bad business to have those people in here. They are usually up to no good. Watch my back if they try anything."

Adam had heard about enough. "So, what are you saying?" he asked. "Are you saying this because she is Black?"

"Let's be real," the lady said. "You know how their kind is."

"No, I actually don't know how their kind is. Care to enlighten me?"

"They are lesser than us, usually speak improperly, are into riffraff things, no good, no jobs, and they just look different from us."

Adam had enough. "I can't listen to this. That's really sad that you think that because not only is it not true but it's wrong. If you got to know them, you would realize that instead of judging and putting them into a box that fits your mindset. No one is all the same. That girl is a lawyer and the best one I know. She's nothing like what you described, and you know what?"

"What?"

"One day I'm going to marry her. She is the most beautiful, amazing, good-hearted woman."

Tara walked over at that moment and said to the lady, "I bet that makes you feel sick, right?" Then she put her arms around Adam's neck and said, "That's right, he's my boyfriend, and we got everything that you just said."

The lady shook her head, told Adam he should be ashamed of himself and is doing a disservice to the White race and to himself, and told them to leave the store. They both felt a wave of emotions.

Monica got it all on recording. "Wow, good job guys, you nailed it," Monica said. "And Adam, I saw the emotion in your face and voice when you added that stuff about how you felt about Tara. Thank you. The whole thing just also just makes me sick, confused, and so angry that this is real. I can't believe it. See, Adam, that's White privilege at its best. Being able to walk into a store like that, never thinking about race and never experiencing anything negative related to it. She treated you great. Wow. I am going to sue and file a report,"

Monica said.

"I am just at a loss for words. It really hurts. That was just crazy. Are we still meeting tonight, Monica?" Tara asked.

"Yeah, we can still go out to dinner. Derek is going to hear a really interesting story. He's going to be like, 'My new girlfriend is a detective now too.'" The girls laughed.

Adam looked at them both. "I'm sorry that happened. I am glad that I could come and help. With that recording, she'll probably be fired, but more than that hopefully she'll change."

"We should pray that she will," Tara said. "So, Adam, you are going to go home and get ready, right? And I'll meet you at your house and then we can go together?"

"Okay, babe. I'll see you ladies later."

The girls were deeply disturbed about what just happened but didn't want it to ruin the night because they knew they'd have fun together with their men. They know how to find the fun, adventure, and thrill in things. They were going to head home and get ready to go out.

As they walked out, Tara said to Monica, "There's something that Adam said that gave me butterflies. He told that lady that one day he is going to marry me. I always wondered if he would ask me one day. We don't really talk about it too much, but I know he loves me, and he does say things that make it sound like he thinks about a future together."

"Yeah, he does, and he's probably just waiting for the right time. It's been a year, right, so there's time but he knows what he wants and has it on his mind, which is good. He is proud of you. That's evident!"

"Oh, I know. He's never hid it in public. We hold hands. He is proud. I know that he doesn't care what anyone thinks."

"He treats you right in every way."

Later that night, the two couples were seated at the restaurant. I asked Tara to send me pictures and she did. The ladies looked beautiful, and the guys looked dapper too.

Adam and Tara formally introduced themselves to Derek and Derek to them. Derek is a tall, bald, big guy with a strong personality. He can be funny at times and pretty stern and outspoken, yet he has a good heart and stands up for what he believes in.

After the intros and sharing about what they do for work, along with some lighthearted, friendly small talk, he said, "So, Monica told me about what happened at the store. That's just crazy, especially to happen to such classy, elegant ladies like yourselves."

"It's really crazy," Adam said.

"What do you know about it?" Derek asked with a slightly defensive, accusatory, and curious tone and look.

"It's okay," Monica said. "He's cool, Derek. I felt the same way in the beginning, but trust me, he's cool. He helped us at the mall."

"I'm sorry man. I'm just on edge, and then I hear about this, and it's too much. I'm sorry. I didn't mean anything by it. You seem cool."

"It reminds me of the time when I was a teenager, and I went with my parents to the Porsche dealer," Tara said. "My dad wanted to get one for my mom, and as soon as we walked in, they said, 'Hello, this is Porsche, big money cars, how can I help you? Are you lost?' My dad asked them what they meant, and he said, 'Oh this is a Porsche dealer, were you looking for something else? There are other dealers on the road. These are high end cars,' he reiterated. Meanwhile, my dad was dressed very nicely, and so was my mom. Usually he's in a suit, but he was dressed a little more down, yet still stylish and professional.

"My dad said, 'I see the game you are trying to play here.' My mom told him they should just leave since they were unwelcome, but my dad insisted that no, he had the money to get a Porsche and wanted one, and it was the closest dealer.

"The guy said okay and that he was just wondering but didn't mean anything by it. He worked with the guy for a while, and he tried to give him an unfair price, but then finally my dad prevailed, and he saw that my dad had enough and more for the car. He underestimated him.

"I'll never forget that experience. I watched my dad stand up in the face of racism and not back down or leave. He asserted himself and said no, I am qualified, I am able, I have the money, and I deserve a seat at the table. Ever since then, I told myself, *Not only do I bring something to the table, I am the table.* Lila and Adam always remind me that's who I am. Sometimes I overcompensate for feeling inadequate or inferior at times.

"My mom taught us to always be proud, and she taught us who we are, not just racially, culturally, but also spiritually, biblically. Both of my parents taught me that, and my dad is on the church board. My mom taught Sunday school. I know that we are all created in God's image, and our different colors and looks are a vast and beautiful representation of creation, of how much bigger and beyond us God is, and he doesn't favor anyone for how they look. I know God loves me, and he has really blessed me in big, unexpected ways. I feel it and I know it."

"I can totally relate, girl," Monica said.

Derek leaned in and shared. "Right, for me being a Black male and a big guy, I'm six-foot-three, I get the stares in White spaces. I get the older ladies clutching their purses when

I reach over their carts to grab something at the supermarket, so I don't even get in the elevator without another male now. I see the people, mostly White women, on the sidewalks scared of me and turn and walk another way when I'm coming toward them, thinking I'm gonna rob or hurt them. I've gotten the racial jokes about being dark and jokes about not showing up in a picture. You have to be proud of who you are and your race.

"It's like you said, Tara. You are the table. I am a Black King," Derek said. "I've never been ashamed of who I am, but when I was younger, yes, sometimes being shunned hurt. Fitting into this box and having assumptions made can sting. Being treated differently because you are Black, not being invited to that birthday party when you are a kid because it's hosted by a White family and you're Black, people being scared of you, that's real.

"Well, Adam, I bet you never felt that or were questioned about if you could afford something because of your race, like that you couldn't afford it when you got your G-Class. It's tough, by the way. I saw it when you pulled up. Very nice. I drive a Benz too."

"Thank you, man," Adam said. "I don't face racism, but I hear you guys. My eyes are open."

"Yeah, man, I know you're cool. Monica told me. I admire that. You guys have been through a lot, and then I know the stuff with your own stuff. I can relate. I have tats too—a sleeve as you can see and some on this arm, a half sleeve, but I'm planning on finishing it. Then I have some on my back and chest too, and you're tatted up too, so we have that in common. I know you faced some stuff with that, and that's different than dealing with racism, but you know, it's something. It's real. It's straight-up judgment and mistreatment. For me, it's a double whammy, but for what I do and, in my spaces, it's pretty much accepted."

The group enjoyed their dinner, laughed, and talked the night away. The guys started talking about different things and life, and they all hit it off. They talked about music and sports too. Adam played hockey, baseball, basketball, and did track and field. Derek did basketball, baseball, and track. The guys connected on many levels and personality-wise.

The waiter came over and asked if they wanted separate checks.

"So, now, why would you say that?" Derek asked. "You don't see that we are together, and they are together? We'll take two checks."

Monica made a lighthearted *here we go* face to Tara with her lips pursed and her head up and Tara smiled.

"Nah, I don't like that though because she is probably asking that 'cause he's White and thinking we aren't couples," Derek said. "Seeing judgments and stereotypes, these things happen. It's a cycle that we need to change. We're not just being sensitive, imagining, or making it up. This stuff happens. We need to be cognizant of our thoughts. They say it doesn't matter what's on the outside, the inside matters, but that's not how all people really see it. The outside is what people look at and view as a scope to the inside, or for some, it just stops there.

"That's why you had the stuff with Madeline," Derek said. "That's why we face all of this stuff. We are presentable, well-dressed, well-kept, hardworking, well-to-do people, but others are going to judge and have their perceptions. The goal is to change that, to get them to realize they need to look deeper than that, because, no, we don't fit their molds or their expectations or assumptions. We are who we are. We are proud of who we are and proud of the skin that we wear, or at least

I know I am, but it's not without its challenges. Sorry for preaching, but this stuff irks me and moves me," Derek said.

"That's for sure. I agree," Monica said.

"Yeah, like Adam," Derek said. "I judged you. When you agreed that it was crazy, I said what do you know about it 'cause you're White, and I know you don't know firsthand. I thought, *what's your place when you don't understand and look like the oppressor?* But no, we want you on our side as an ally. It's a good thing. It's how change comes when we fight together. It's awesome that you're in it.

"I judged Monica. I think she's beautiful and someone that I wanted to get to know, and it goes beyond that. We see the outside, but what do we do with that? Does it set the tone? Do we treat someone differently or even think differently about them? Our thoughts matter, and so do our perceptions. Even if we don't like or agree with something, even if what we do or believe is different, respect is crucial. It's a must. Sometimes judgment comes from ignorance or lack of education and understanding. Sometimes people just don't realize or didn't mean to, and I get that. That's why we have to set the tone."

"I hear you, you're right," Adam said.

"Most definitely, it's something to think about for sure. Naturally, as people, we are going to think things and judge, and sometimes that could be good to help us avoid bad things, but we need to really think about our thoughts and why we have them. We have to be better at discerning," Derek said. "Let's do better as people, so that we don't even give a reason to these people who want to judge us. Collectively do better so that we can be seen for who we really are in a different and good light across the board, not exceptions, not the minority of it. We can't control what people think or, sadly, sometimes how they see us, but we can try to shift the mindsets by being ourselves, just putting that out there."

"That was insightful, Derek. Thank you for sharing that. It's so true, and it's already got me thinking," Tara said.

"Thanks for coming to my TED Talk," Derek said as they all laughed playfully. As they wrapped up the evening, Derek told Adam that they should get together. The group said their goodbyes and left. They were thankful for a great time. Both couples said to each other that it was fun when they got into the car.

Tara and Adam listened to music and sang on the ride home. They headed back to Adam's house. When they got there, they got into sweats, and Adam had a tank top on. Tara had sweats and a hoodie on. They sat on the couch by the TV. Tara had her legs and feet up on Adam's lap.

Tara asked Adam if he had a good time.

"For sure, it was fun," Adam said. "Did you?"

"Yeah, I did. What do you think about Derek?"

"He's insightful, he's cool."

"He has a strong personality, right?" Tara said.

"He does," Adam said, "but he's funny. I like him. Nice guy, and we have a lot of similar interests. We might go to this ninja warrior gym obstacle course. I'm stoked".

"That's fun," Tara said.

"Yeah. He's into fitness too. That and CrossFit."

"Well, good babe. That's right up your alley. You'll have to tell him about your healthy veggie meal ideas and stuff you eat: your kale, chia seeds, oat, fruit smoothies you make, how you're really into health with the occasional cheat meal, and sweets like me," she said with a playful smile.

"I will," he said playfully.

Tara looked at him and blushed.

"What?" he asked.

"I just can't believe you're mine." Her stomach melted and the butterflies took over as his gorgeous, bright-blue eyes shined into hers, and his muscular arms and figure made her feel like she was in a dream world. Most of all, it's the look and expression he makes with his eyes and face that really gets her when he holds his head up, looks down, and makes this side smile. That, topped with the person he is inside, makes her so grateful to be his and for him to be hers.

"I love you, Tara Bear," he said. "Ever since I saw you at De La Lina, when you walked in, and I served you, and then we started talking every time you came back. I loved how you would come in every week to talk. You were the prettiest girl in the room and still are."

"I love how it grew from there when you asked me for my number, and then we started talking for hours and hanging out, then you asked me to be your girlfriend," Tara said.

"I am so grateful for you," Adam told her. He asked her if she wanted to watch a movie.

"I'd love to. I'm just gonna get some hot tea. You want some, babe?"

"Sure," he said. She got it and they scrolled through to find a movie that they wanted to watch. They enjoyed their evening and went in the hot tub after the movie. They planned a bike ride, the beach, and seeing live music for the next day. I enjoyed texting with Tara about what she was up to and about what I was up to.

Chapter 7

I was back from my outings and back at De La Lina. Tara filled me in on everything that had happened, so I felt like I was a part of it.

"Hey Adam!"

"Lila, what's up!" he said enthusiastically. "How was your time away?"

"It was a lot of fun, thanks."

"That's awesome," he said.

"Have you guys been holding down the fort without me?"

"We have, but you know it's not the same without you, Lila. Great to have you back. Tara missed you too."

"I know. I missed her. We texted."

"She told me."

"Oh, Adam, Madeline is over there."

"Okay, we'll talk," Adam said.

Mike went up to Adam and said, "Hey, Madeline requested you."

Adam went over to Madeline and asked how she was.

She said that she was doing really well and asked how he was. She told him that she was there on her lunch break. Adam is always the waiter who she requests now. She even told Mike that Adam is the best server. He is fast, attentive, polite, professional, friendly, and works hard, she said. She tells all of her friends to request him—not to mention the food at De La Lina is really good. Adam was appreciative. He served her well.

Adam, Tara, Branson, and I have plans after work tomorrow to go to the park to do some outdoor activities, and then go downtown, walk around, shop, and hear live music, so that is something that I am really looking forward to with my fun crew. Monica might join us too. Things with Branson have been going really well.

Later that night, Adam, Tara, Branson, and I met at Adam's parents' house for dinner. Before we enjoyed a nice meal together, Adam's dad went to do some reading in his study for work, and his mom and us sat on the couch to talk.

"So how are you guys doing?" Tammy asked us.

"Good!"

"We're good," we said. "How are you?"

"Good. I know, you guys met with some friends for a double date. How was that?"

"It was good," Tara said. "We got to talk about our experiences, life, interests, work, and just bond. We talked about what happened at the mall."

"Yes, your mom told me about that," Tammy said.

"She told me," Tara said.

"She called me, and she said what had happened with that. She was disturbed, of course, as was I," Tammy continued.

"Yeah, it's hard."

Tammy leaned in. "That reminds me that I wanted to talk to you guys about something. I went out recently to a play with one of my friends and her friend's friend came. We went to the play, and it was a good show. We enjoyed it. The conversations were light in line and before the play started. It was my first time meeting this lady. Not my friend's friend, but her friend.

"So, after the play, we go out to dinner, and we're talking about the play, our families, and small talk, and she makes a racist comment. I was taken aback. I'm thinking, like, okay, did she really just say this? She's at a table full of White women and probably thinks that we all accept that or agree with that type of thinking. So, she goes on, and it was, like, did I hear that right or understand that right? It was racism, and it was disparaging.

"So, she continues on and says some bad things about Black people and other minorities, and then says, 'If my child ever brought one home, I'd be livid. I'd disown them.' At this point it's personal for me. My friend was looking at me, and I could tell that she felt embarrassed because she knows.

"I say, 'What would be bad about that? What if they treated your child better than a White person, or they loved them and had fun with the person?' She was saying that it was too different and would repulse her. She actually used that word. I was beside myself. I lost my appetite. I told her, 'My son is dating a girl who happens to be Black, and she is a very lovely girl who my husband and I really like for our son and like in general as a person. She is a lawyer, from a great family. She's pretty and is a really good person,' I told her. She blatantly told me that she has no idea how I do it and aren't I embarrassed? She told me that I shouldn't tolerate that and did something wrong to allow it. She also said that she could never truly accept that and that she didn't get it.

"I excused myself from the dinner. I knew there was no getting through to her. I couldn't be around that. I put down the money for what my meal cost, and I told my friend I had to go but would call her later. I called my sister Janine on the car ride home and Chuck on a three-way, and I was just really upset.

"I was contemplating if I should even tell you guys about this because it is offensive, it's hurtful, and I hope it is okay that I brought this up. I am so embarrassed to sit here now and to be even saying that this is real life and that this happened. She felt a level of comfort being at a table full of

White women thinking that this dialogue would be okay, and not only is it wrong but I am personally offended by it. I told Janine, I said, 'This is wrong on so many levels', and she said 'Yes, it is, and it offends you even more because of your son's girlfriend, and she's your buddy on top of that.'

"You know I love you, Tara. You are like a second daughter to me, and I love you for my son and as a person," Tammy sighed, and tears rolled down her face.

"Don't cry, Mom. You stood up, and you were really bold. I'm really glad that you did that," Adam said.

"Tara, I am so sorry for everything that you face as a Black woman, and you too, Lila. You are a great friend to them. It's hard. I am so sorry from the bottom of my heart. What I can do, is what I often wonder," she said as she wiped her eyes.

Tara reached over and took Tammy's hand and said, "Everything that you are doing. Calling out racism when you see it—not being okay or comfortable with that. Treating me and other people with respect and dignity, you are doing it all. Thinking about it and being exposed to diverse groups is also really good. Also, Adam gets it from somewhere. You did good."

"We raised our kids to not judge by color. I mean, they see it because everyone sees it, but not to treat people differently because of color or to judge them and to just treat everyone the same and get to know people for who they are as a person and their character. We taught Adam and Jenny to never think that they were better than anyone else, and we wanted to expose them to different cultures. They always befriended anyone regardless and never cared about that," Tammy replied.

"You have done a really good job with that, Tammy. You raised an amazing man. He's a free thinker in ways. He's compassionate. You are doing the best that you can do," Tara said.

Tammy smiled. "Thank you. I love you guys. Ever since he brought you home, I took to you. We just click. I'm going to tell my friend about her friend's friend and just where I stand."

"Thank you for that, Tammy. I love you too." They hugged, and Adam thanked his mom, hugged her, and then reached his arms around to embrace and pull in Tara. He gave her a kiss on the forehead. He brought me in for a group hug too.

By now, Chuck was done with his reading. He came out and saw the emotion. "What did I miss?" he asked.

We laughed. "Let's eat and then start the movie," I said.

Adam's mom told us that she was so happy that Branson and I connected. She's known Branson for years, loves him, and gets along well with his parents. Adam and Chuck fell asleep during the movie, and Tara did for a little bit and then woke up. Branson and I ended up mostly whispering through the movie.

When Tara woke up, she talked to Tammy about the mall incident and how Adam told the worker that he was going to marry her one day. She told Tammy that she told her mom about it and was excited to hear him say that because they never discussed it really. She asked Tammy if she thinks he said it to make the lady in the store mad or if it was something he meant and thought of.

Tammy told her that Adam meant it because he doesn't say things that he doesn't mean, especially things that carry that weight. It was getting late, and Tammy asked us all if we wanted to sleep over. Tara doesn't live far, but it was getting late, and she thought it would be fun. We agreed to stay, and she set us up in the guest room. Branson took the couch.

The next morning, after Adam got ready, he went into the kitchen by his mom. He hugged her, gave her a kiss on the cheek, and thanked her for what she said and did. He told her that he was grateful for her support and the way that she loves his girlfriend.

His dad walked in. "Hey, your mom is pretty great. That's why I made her mine when she was sixteen and I was seventeen. Adam, you've always been your own man, and we are proud of you. You're a grown man and can choose to make your own decisions, and you know we love and support you in those. We'll always back you."

"Thanks Dad, love you," he said. They shared a special family moment, and Tara went down and joined them.

She then came to sit with me on the couch where I was reading. I was feeling butterflies of how perfectly things were going with Branson. I love the way he makes me feel, our conversations and always enjoy spending time with him. Getting to know him and who he is has been a great adventure for me, plus he's really eye catching. My family embraces him too and welcomes and enjoys the time we spend together. My parents are loving and caring. We value our close relationship.

Chapter 8

Later that day, at De La Lina, Adam and I observed a customer who was sitting at the bar. He looked like he had a lot going on, honestly. I asked Mike to go check on him.

"Hey buddy, you alright?" Mike asked. "You look kinda drowsy."

"Oh, yeah, I'm good."

"Okay, bud," he said, "Well, just want to make sure that you're okay. Let me know if you need anything." Mike made a cut gesture to the bartender to say not to pour him any more drinks.

I told Adam that when he gets a moment, maybe he can try to talk to the guy.

"Hey, what's up man?" he said, "I'm Adam."

The guy looked up at him and nodded.

"What's your name?" Adam asked.

"I'm Dean."

Adam asked him how his night was going.

"My night is going okay," Dean said.

"You sure?" Adam asked.

"Well, not really. I just lost my job a couple days ago."

"Oh, I'm sorry to hear that."

"Yeah, you know, stupid stuff, man."

"I'm sorry to hear that. That's rough," Adam said.

"Yeah, what can you do?"

"What did you do for work?" Adam asked him.

"I sold insurance, but I've been having some family issues lately, and it's been hard to focus on work. I've just been going through some stuff, dude. Cool tats by the way. I have one on my shoulder and one on my leg. I might get more."

"That's cool, man, for sure," Adam said.

"You have an artist already?" Adam asked.

"Yeah, yeah, cool guy, reputable place."

"That's good. My guy uses high standards too."

"Yeah, man. Well, I'm gonna jet," Dean said. "Catch you next time, Adam. My friend is here to pick me up."

Adam nodded and finished up his work duties and then went to Tara's house. Before he left, we were all saying that we were glad the guy didn't drive there, and if he had, we would have had to intervene.

Tara picked up some food for Adam. The next day, he was off from De La Lina, so he volunteered as a firefighter, worked out, and then met up with Tara later. Tara and I had spent the day together. We were then going to meet up for a double date dinner.

They dressed up and got into his G-Class. They were driving along when Adam saw a car speeding past them.

"Oh my gosh!" Tara exclaimed. "That's crazy! Where could they be going that fast?" Adam shared her sentiments as they watched the road.

Then they saw another car doing the same thing. The first car was way ahead of them, but they saw it crash into a tree on the side of the road. Adam pulled the car over when they got closer.

"What are you doing?" Tara asked him.

"Checking to see if they're okay. Stay in the car, Tara."

Tara was texting me as this was happening. Adam got out of the car and opened the door on the driver's side. The guy was alert but bleeding a little bit and had some cuts.

"Ahh," the guy said.

"Are you okay?" Adam asked him.

"Yeah, I think so," he said.

"Have you been drinking?"

"I had one drink, man, maybe two."

"Your car reeks of alcohol. I'm going to call 911. Get you some help."

"Great," the guy said sarcastically, "thanks. You've got to be kidding me."

Adam waited with the guy, and Tara watched from the car with her seatbelt tightly fastened. She locked the doors and had a concerned look on her face.

Adam looked at him and said, "Dean, right?"

"Yeah, you're the guy from that restaurant. What's your name again?"

"Adam."

The police showed up. Dean refused an ambulance, saying he was fine. His blood alcohol content was sky high. He got a DUI that night.

The next day, Adam, Tara, and I went to meet with Dean. We met with him at a tea shop, and Adam told him that he was worried about him, how he was at De La Lina, how he crashed and then got a DUI. He told him that we just wanted to help.

Tara looked concerned for him and nodded in agreement with Adam.

I did too. I made small talk with Dean and let him know that he could trust us.

Dean opened up to us and told us that he lost his job and that he's been struggling. He said that at age fifteen he found out that he was adopted. Now at age thirty-one he just met his half-brother on his dad's side, which has been hard. It was exciting at first, but it has been hard to build that sibling bond and connection at this age when so much time has already passed and they did not grow up together.

He told us that he resented his parents for not telling him about the adoption sooner and that he wrestles with thoughts of being unwanted by his birth parents. He said that being different in that way really affected him and has been hard, and while his adoptive parents have been loving, kind, and have taken care of him, when he saw other families, he wished that he could have that and share blood with his parents.

He said that some nights he cries in his room about his feelings of being unwanted and unloved. He said though that he understands why his birth mother gave him up and that he thinks it was the right decision based on her circumstances. He was able to meet her once, but she is not consistent in wanting a relationship with him, and neither is his birth father. He deals with feelings about it all and self-esteem issues. He sometimes gets jealous of his friends' families and other people when they have their real parents in their lives, and he has a reminder that he was unwanted. But he said that he is grateful to be adopted by a good family.

"I am so sorry," Tara said. "That has got to be hard."

I told him that I was sorry too, and Adam said, "We are here for you. We all have our hardships and things that make us feel unworthy, but you can get through this. It's not your fault, and it wasn't your choice to be adopted, but what you can do is make choices that you can be proud of now. I'm sorry that you went through that and are feeling those feelings."

I told Dean that God cares and that "Those who hope in the Lord will renew their strength."

Dean shook his head as to say he acknowledged what I said and said thank you. He said that those sound like nice and calming verses that he would read.

"Can we do anything to help?" I asked him. "You guys being here right now is everything. No one really cares about me that much to stop what they are doing and have this intervention, especially people that I just met. Talking to me at De La Lina, and then you, Adam, getting out of the car has been life changing. I was mad at first that you called 911, but I'm glad you did.

"It was the right thing to do not just for my own safety physically but because it was a wakeup call for me. Being out of control like that isn't something that I want anymore. I don't want to hurt myself or anyone else more importantly. That feeling when I'm drunk isn't something that I want anymore. It just makes me sick and feel worse. I don't want to live just for the moment anymore.

"I am going to stop drinking. My goal is for a month, and then I am going to go from there and gradually into every month. I don't want that life any longer. I realize the severity of my actions that could not only impact my life but the lives of others."

"That's good," we all chimed in. "We are here for you, Dean, anything you need. When you need to talk, need support, or someone else out with you, we will never force or ask you to drink or be drinking around you. We don't really drink anyway. Whatever you need, we are your people," Tara said.

"Thank you so much," Dean said. "I am super grateful for you guys. So excited to have met you."

We all hugged and went home. Adam and Tara dropped me home and then went back to her parents' house, where they were going to be sleeping over for the night to spend time with Charles and Denise. Tara said that she would text me later. They arrived at the house and Denise welcomed them in with hugs. The four of them sat on the couch.

"How are you guys?" Denise asked.

"Good, Mom," Tara said.

"Good, thank you, Ms. Denise," Adam said.

"I hear you guys are in the business of helping people," Charles said.

"It's mostly Adam, Dad. It's just who he is."

"I see that. I know you are humble, Adam, and don't do it for the accolades, but you do deserve a thank you. It is something to be proud of, and your friend Lila is also a very good person. She inspires people."

"I know for sure she has inspired me to be better, to be my best self, and to be more like God," Adam said.

"That's the most important thing, Adam, and it's all that matters at the end," Charles said.

"How are your parents, Adam?" Denise asked.

"They are good, thank you. They are working on the garden today. They are always asking about you guys too."

"Very nice. Tell them hello for us."

"I will, thank you."

Denise said that she was going to invite his parents to a couples' tea party event at their church and that she thinks they would like it. The foursome enjoyed the rest of the evening, talking, laughing, and enjoying good conversation and movies. Adam and Chuck went to bed, and before Tara went to bed, her mom Denise came into her room. "Goodnight pumpkin, love bug, Tara Bara," she said.

"Mom," Tara said, "I really love Adam."

"I know you do, and believe me, he loves you too. I see it in his eyes, in how he treats you. He's a keeper, honey."

"I am so glad that you guys like him."

"Yeah, at first we were thinking that it was different, or we were a little unsure of how things would play out with him and who he is, but as we got to know him, we quickly changed. Once you talk to Adam for a few minutes how could you not like him?"

"Thank you, Mom." They said their goodnights.

The next day, Adam and Branson went to the gym to lift weights. Tara and I were there too on the treadmills, admiring our men in the mirror with their dashing good looks. Branson and I just started dating.

Derek soon joined them by the weights with one of his gym friends, Trevor, who just got back from visiting family in Puerto Rico.

"What's up man?" they all said. Derek was telling Trevor that he and his new girlfriend, Monica, who things are going well with, went on a double date with Adam and his girlfriend Tara. He told him that before the date, Monica and Tara faced racism in the mall that Adam helped them with.

"Oh, okay. That was nice of you and Tara to help Monica deal with a racist experience," Trevor said. "It's hard, and Adam, your girlfriend got to see what racism was like by being out with a Black friend."

Adam made a confused expression, and Derek jumped in and said, "His girlfriend is Black too."

"Oh, okay, so it's like that. I didn't know you got down like that. I see you." Then he nodded his head and pointed to Adam with his finger shaking and with a smile on his face. Adam smiled. "Tara is amazing. I'm really blessed to have her," he said and then he lifted some weights.

Trevor glanced over. "If you don't mind my asking, as a White dude, was it the first time out of your race, or was it different for you getting with a Black girl?"

Adam kept his weights going. "I dated two girls a while before her who were both White, and then I talked to a girl once before her for a little bit who was half Peruvian and another culture, but being with Tara wasn't different for me.

It wasn't something that I thought that much about. I saw her at De La Lina and right away I thought that she was really beautiful, and once we started talking, and she came back week after week, we clicked. I knew that there was a connection between us. She loved to come and talk to me, and I loved talking to her too. I asked her for her number, and we texted. I would call. I pursued her, I asked her out, and it went from there. We went on some dates and then eventually I asked her to be my girlfriend. I asked her three months into knowing her, and now we've been together for a year. It never really felt different for me."

"Right, that's awesome man, I imagined it might have some challenges to overcome with the presence of seeing race," Trevor said.

"She's a woman, and I do acknowledge and know that she's Black, because obviously I see it. She has faced racism, so, for me, I'm aware of that and have been there for her. In that regard, it was something new to me because, as a White man, I don't face racism, right? But being there for her through that, learning, listening, and understanding, has opened my eyes to what other people go through and what that is like. But in the aspect of our relationship, race was never anything that made anything different between us. It's just what happens outside of our relationship. There are little things culturally that she tells me about and then also her being Jamaican is cool 'cause I've really gotten into the food and the culture, the music. I love the accent too."

"Right, right, makes sense, that's great," Trevor said. "Sounds like you're a good man, Adam, that's what's up. I love that. How about you, Branson, dating a Black girl too?" Trevor asked.

"I am. She's half Black, half Samoan, and she's

friends with Adam and Tara too. They are both over there on the treadmills." Just then their conversation got cut off.

"Hi, excuse me," said a girl who came up to Adam, Branson, and Derek. "What made you guys get all those tattoos? What does it mean? Did it hurt? Are you going to get anymore?" She asked one by one. Then she proceeded to touch Adam.

"Woah, woah, woah," Trevor said with a *chill out* kind of look before Adam could answer. "Please leave the man alone. We are working out."

"I'm sorry," the girl said flirtatiously, and then she left.

"That was just weird," Trevor said. "Does that happen a lot man?"

"Yeah, people ask me those questions all the time, and some people, mostly girls, come up and touch me. I just say ouch or make a joke like that when they do it."

"It doesn't bother you?"

"I've had tattoos for nine years now, so I try to just let it go. Sometimes it can be a lot with the touching though, but I'm heavily tattooed right? So, people are going to ask questions and some touch. Sometimes, when I tell people that I work at a restaurant, they say, 'Oh, in the back?' Maybe because of my neck tattoos, and they are surprised to hear that I serve. It's funny when people touch me though because the tattoos don't feel like anything. It just feels like regular skin."

"Yeah, that's crazy bro. So you just get it from every direction? Tats, racism with your lady, and I hear you do volunteer firefighting and teach fitness?"

"Yeah, it's rewarding work. I'm thinking about opening my own fitness studio too. I am also interested in some other things, so we'll see. I love the outdoors, doing nature stuff, and playing sports."

"That's awesome man," he said, "really cool."

"Thanks. What do you do?"

"I work for a phone company."

They carried on talking and enjoyed conversation at the gym and lifting.

Tara and I said bye to our guys and then headed out to the beach. We love the water, sunshine, trees, and nature. We are so blessed to be surrounded by breathtaking views all around us and have a beautiful day ahead of us. We had movie and dinner plans at a nice new plaza for that evening by the mall.

Adam had an interesting story for us later.

Later that day, Adam and Chuck were in the hardware store and ran into Dean and his mom, Lori.

"Adam!" he said enthusiastically, "how are you?"

"Good, man. This is my dad, Chuck."

"Oh, nice to meet you. This is my mom, Lori.

"Nice to meet you too."

"This is the guy who saved me that night when I crashed."

"Oh wow," Lori said. "Thank you so much for what you did. You're a hero. He was really spiraling, and had it not been for your interventions that night, it could have been much worse. He really learned his lesson."

"No problem. I am glad to hear that. How've you been?" Adam asked Dean.

"I've been great. They dropped the DUI charge down to reckless driving, but I know that it was a DUI in my mind. I haven't been drinking at all, and I don't miss it or ever want to go back to it. I got a new job too at a tile and upscale furniture store as a salesperson, so I'm doing that for now. It's right next to an electronics store. Things have been better, and I'm in counseling for my issues that I told you about."

"Wow man, that's really good news. I'm glad that you learned and that you are on a good path."

"I can't thank you enough, Adam, for stopping that night, talking to me. You changed my life. Just caring and helping me changed the course of my life. Even though I didn't see it at that moment, calling 911 and getting that charge was a huge wake-up call to do and be better. It takes time, but I'm doing much better."

"I am glad to hear that," Adam said.

"We are so appreciative for everything that you did, Adam. Maybe we could take you guys out for dinner to thank you," Lori said. "Or you guys are welcome to come over for dinner tomorrow night. My wife is a great cook," Chuck said.

"That sounds wonderful," Lori said. "Tomorrow it is. I'll tell my husband, Dave."

The next day, Lori, Dave, and Dean got ready to go over to Chuck and Tammy's house. Adam was there, and Tara would arrive a little bit later.

"Can I help you with anything, Mom?" Adam asked her.

"I'm good. Just please put some napkins on the table. So, this guy, Dean, is the guy you helped with the car crash, DUI?"

"Yes, Dad and I ran into him and his mom at the store, and they wanted to do dinner to say thank you, and Dad said that they could come over. Dean is doing much better now."

"That's good, honey. I'm so proud of you, as always. Tara is coming over later, right?"

"Yes, she's doing some work, and then she's going to

come."

"Okay, oh, there they are. Get the door, Adam, and I'll be right out."

Adam and Chuck went to open the door and greet their guests. Tammy came out with a dish of carrots to put on the table, and as she was about to say hello, she saw Dean and his parents and dropped the dish. The dish broke and glass and the carrots scattered.

"Lori, what are you doing here?" Tammy asked her.

"I'm Dean's mom. I didn't know this was your house. So, you're Adam's mom?"

"Yes, I am. This is my husband, Chuck, and this is our house."

Adam, Chuck, Dean, and Lori's husband all looked confused.

"Did I miss something?" Chuck asked.

"So, you two know each other?" asked Lori's husband, Dave.

"Yeah, we do," Lori said. "Maybe we should go. I had no idea that Tammy was your mom."

"Wait," Chuck said, "what is going on and how do you know each other?"

"She's the friend of my friend's friend that I told you about. We went to a play together and dinner, and, honestly, she had some things to say which I took offense to. They were very offensive things, especially because of Tara, and here we are now. My son saved her son, and I had no idea it was her son."

"Oh my gosh, Lori how could you do that?" Dave said. "I told you to keep that to yourself. Look, we can leave if you would like."

"You know what, it's okay," Tammy said.

Adam helped clean things up and met his mom in the kitchen.

"Adam, do you think you should tell Tara not to come over? I don't want her exposed to racism, especially not under my roof."

"I'll call her and see what she wants to do."

After they got off the phone, Adam told Tammy that Tara was going to come over. When Tara arrived, her and Adam exchanged a kiss and a hug.

The dinner was awkward but also manageable. The men carried the conversation with their love of golf, work talk, and other conversations. Tammy and Lori were more on the quiet side although Tammy was talking to Adam and Tara. Dean and his parents thanked Adam again for what he did, and the dinner ended, and the family left.

"You can't win them all, Mom," Adam said. "Some people will change, and some won't. It doesn't matter what she thinks about me or us. I'm proud to be with Tara. She's the best thing that has happened to me. She fills my life."

"I know sweetie. At least she didn't say anything offensive today, and she didn't even mention your tattoos, which was good," Tammy said.

"Yeah, she didn't want to add insult to injury," Adam said. "Thanks for always supporting, accepting, and loving me in everything, Mom. Sorry about all the tattoos, Mom, but glad you never got too mad over it," he said playfully.

"Of course," Tammy said. "You were always a wildfire. We accept that. We love you. You kept us on our toes."

The next day, Adam and Tara were heading out to meet Derek and Monica for a double date. I had to work at De La Lina that night, but we were going to go out soon too. They were meeting at a rooftop restaurant downtown with a nice firepit. The guys were dressed nice and sharp as always, and the ladies were both stunning. They were gentlemen and held the door for the ladies.

Monica filled me in on how the night went. There was another couple sitting by them whom they got into a conversation with. The couple was a little tipsy and said to Tara, "How can you be pro Black and recognize the place you hold in society when you are booed up with a White dude? You have to support your race in all things. Buy Black, combat racism, and as a White dude, he simply can't begin to understand what we go through. Loving someone that intimately isn't something that I could do. The respect, trust, and understanding just wouldn't be there for me."

"First of all," Derek said as he jumped in with his lips pursed and head moving around, "you guys have had too much to drink, so you aren't thinking clearly. Sit down. Me and my crew, we haven't. I personally don't drink much anymore. Too many bad experiences for me personally, and we like to be in control of our mind and our actions, not getting carried away with drinking. And we like to be aware of our surroundings and not feel lightheaded. Plus, for us, we stay having fun. We don't need that. It doesn't add to it for us. Just not interested.

"This is one of those times when you need to step back 'cause you're insulting my friends, and clearly you guys don't get it. You don't know them or what they've been through, and when I tell you this White dude is cool, he's down, I mean it," Derek said.

"Babe, Adam can defend his lady," Monica said to Derek.

"I know he can, but you know how I am. I'm loud, I'm bold, I can be hotheaded and passionate. I don't like this, so I'm going to say something, plus Adam is my bro."

Tara jumped in. "So, I can't be pro Black and love a White man? Why does pro Black and proud of being Black have to be anti-something else or anti-White? I can love and be with him and still appreciate and support my race and the struggles that my people have been through. I'm a lawyer. A Black, female lawyer. I know what it means to be Black and to feel that. I'm Black and a woman. I'm proud."

"Well," the girl said, "all I could see in him is being White, and no matter how good looking or how nice and caring he is, he can't understand what it means to be Black. But you do you. Keep being with the enemy. That's fine for you, and I know that some people do support it or encourage it, but I am just not one of them. I am against it. I am for the Black family. I love Black men and Black love.

"He doesn't deserve a Black queen," said the girl.

"He does deserve a Black queen, and I give him props because he respects her and treats her like a queen. He values her and treats her right, so he is deserving of her," Derek said.

Tara became emotional mentally but didn't want to cry. Her thoughts flooded her like a flashback or a fast movie reel. All she could think about were the times when Adam sat with her when she was facing racism at work and when she faced racism at the concert and felt so small and inferior. She thought of how he sat there in the car and waited, and his presence in that moment meant everything when she was too defeated to even speak or articulate how she was feeling. How he was there for her when she wanted to leave Utah. How he drove her to the Pacific Coast Highway to tell her about something sentimental, and how he felt about her to make her feel special and have her see herself the way that he saw her. He did it to cheer her up and share his feelings. All the times he took her out and how he always made her feel. All the times he listened to her. The times when they just sat on the couch and talked. The adventures, the bike rides, the exploring, sightseeing, the bands they saw and sports games. All the places by the water that they went. The nature, beach, water parks and just the love that he showed her every day. She was at her breaking point.

She stood up. "So what that's he's White?" Tara said. "So we aren't supposed to be together? It's supposed to be a struggle? Are we so unlikely? For what? 'Cause of our races? Are we too different because he's tatted and I'm not? Because it seems like it's always the outside that matters and never the inside? If you knew all of the things he's done not just for me but for so many people. If you saw the way that he makes me laugh—the pure joy that I feel in those moments, the butterflies I feel when he just looks at me, when we drive and we sing along to the music. When he holds my hand, he sacrifices himself to help everyone else. He literally runs into danger.

"He is an incredible human being. Who are you to make me for a second feel bad about loving someone who happens to be White. Did he choose to be White? Can he change it? And you know what? I am attracted to him. I think he's hot and he's attracted to me too. He has made me a better person, been there for me, and we connect on a deep level. He is not racist, and just because he is White doesn't mean you should group him with people that really are racist and have been. He actively tries to understand even though he can't know what it is like to be Black and doesn't have that perspective. That doesn't make him bad. It's not a reason for me to not love him, 'cause I can't imagine not loving him."

For the first time, Tara saw Adam's eyes teary. For the first time, he was also speechless. Monica was looking at everyone's faces, and Derek was too.

"I'm done," Tara said as she walked away.

Adam followed behind.

"T!" Monica shouted as she trailed behind. "You okay?"

"Yeah, why don't you guys just come back to my house?" Tara said.

"Okay, we'll meet you there. We'll just go change, and then we will be there."

"Okay, sounds good," Tara said.

Adam and Tara got into his G-class. The car ride started out quiet. Tara looked over at Adam driving and saw a tear fall down his face.

"Adam, are you okay?"

"Yeah, babe. I appreciate everything you said. It touched me. I know it's hard."

"We'll talk about it later, babe," Tara said.

They got to her house, and when Derek and Monica arrived, they made hot chai and had a pillow fight on the couch. Tara just wanted to forget what happened and let her hair down. They made the best of the night on their own terms and laughed. It ended up being a lighthearted night. When I got off my shift, Branson and I joined them in the fun of the night. Our guys can be really funny and chill at the same time. The nonchalant kind of funny and fun when you're not trying to be is the best kind. We played games and didn't mind the clock. Things are going well with Branson and I dating. We are taking it slow.

The next day, Tara's aunt, Tatiana, went over to Tara's. Tatiana is one of her dad's younger sisters, and Tara and Tatiana are pretty close. When she walked in, they hugged and sat on the couch.

"So, what's going on? How's Adam?" she asked.

"He's good. He's working at De La Lina today, taught fitness before and then he has his volunteer work after."

"Okay, he's busy. You guys okay, though?"

"Yeah, Aunt Tati. Sometimes it is just hard with the things we go through with racism, but I love him and he's great. He loves the Lord."

Tatiana squeezed her hand. "That's all that matters," she said. "You're strong, you're smart, you're resilient, and you can handle it. He's a good man. A strong, caring man. I think it's worth it, and I am here for you through it all, Tara. You are my niece, and I love you. I really like Adam. He's a wonderful guy. Your dad and your mom told me about how he has been there for you, and he's consistently good. They like him. His parents like you, right?"

"Yeah, I'm pretty close with his mom especially. She's really nice, they both are."

"Good. Well don't let what people say bring you down or stop you from fully loving this man just like you never let any obstacles stop you from anything. From the time you were a little girl to dancing ballet, you never gave up. You always had ambition and drive. You had dreams. You're a boss babe. You would even tell your Barbies not to give up as a child and created great stories with them. I never want to see that shine taken, Tara.

"I remember how proud of you your dad was when you were born and ever since. Unspeakable love and joy filled him. He will always be proud of you. You're a smart, talented, beautiful, driven lawyer, and Black woman. I say that because we know the stereotypes and hardships, the internal and external struggles, so I say it's something for you to be proud of."

"Thank you, Aunt Tatiana. You always know what to say." They hugged and smiled.

🌿 Chapter 9

The next day when Tara was leaving work, she got a call from Adam.

"What's up, babe?"

"Hey, Tara Bear. How are you?

"Good babe, how are you?" Tara said.

"Good, I talked to Dean earlier, and he said that he is doing well. Staying sober, living, and enjoying life. He said that it feels good to be in control of things, instead of things being in control of him and to be in control of his life and decisions. He said people ask him why he doesn't drink anymore, or some people try to ask him to just have one. It makes him feel pressured at times and annoyed that they feel the need to tell him or question him, but he knows that within him it isn't something that he misses, needs, or wants to do anymore. He just doesn't desire it. It's not something that he craves or thinks enhances his life in any way anymore.

He told me that he views it as a social poison that brings destruction more often than not. Not that at times he couldn't control his intake but that it is powerful enough to control him, and he would get carried away. He told me that each choice in life reveals in you the person who you are, or maybe who you always were, could be, or are meant to be. It got me thinking about life and struggles. The ones we have faced but the people who have had and have it worse than us.

"This guy that I met years ago and kept in contact with—his name is Myles—came to my mind for some reason."

"I think you might have mentioned him before. Where did you guys meet?" Tara asked.

"We met at a tattoo convention in Seattle about five

years ago. He was a cool guy, and I haven't talked to him in maybe three years, but for some reason he came to my mind late last night, and it was this nagging feeling that I couldn't ignore, so I told myself that I would call or text him this morning, and I did.

"Babe, he told me that when I called him he was sitting in an empty dirt and gravel parking lot facing a river and woods with two bottles of pills, and had already taken three pills, and was ready to take the rest."

"Oh my," Tara said.

"He told me that he prayed and said, 'God, if you are real, show me a sign. Tell me what to do.' And then I called, he said, within a minute or two. He told me that he remembered when we met at the tattoo convention and that I was nice to him. He said that my words there to him really made a difference in his life—how I encouraged him and motivated him in different areas of his life—but that he has had some setbacks that triggered pain inside of him, and he has been battling some issues. He said that he couldn't believe that I was calling out of nowhere and that I was the sign from God that he needed. I had no idea how I had even impacted him those years ago."

"Wow, that's God!" Tara said.

"You know what's crazy, Tara? When I talked to Lila yesterday, she told me that she prayed once for God to give someone close to her, who is godly, a dream about what she should do in a particular situation. And she never told the person that, but the person told her the next day that they had a dream, and it was so specific to her. She knew what the right thing to do in that situation was. It reminds me of this because I just got a feeling to call this guy, and I call him in the middle of a suicide attempt."

"Wow, that's amazing. So crazy. So what happened?" Tara asked.

"So, he lives in Nevada, and I stayed with him on the phone and called his local police. They picked him up and took him to hospital for treatment. He's coming here next week, and I'm going to talk to him more."

"I am glad you did. What triggered this for him, Adam?"

"He said it was thoughts of not being good enough. Thoughts of people judging him throughout his life. When he was little, his stepdad beat him sometimes, and as an adult, he has always had a hard time with being accepted. He also never really fit into his family. His mom wasn't always there for him. She was abused, and he didn't get the love that he needed in his family life and dynamic. He felt that he was never really wanted and was often put down. For him, that set the tone to his life, coming from a broken family where his dad was sometimes in the picture but not there as a dad should be, and not together with his mom was hard. His stepdad having some drinking issues and his mother not being as present or together as a mother should be, especially for the sake of the kids, was hard for him."

"Wow, that's really heavy," Tara said. "We should invite him to church. That could really help him. For him to find that grace, love, courage, acceptance, and strength would be so assuring and amazing. The trajectory of his life could change."

"I agree," Adam said.

Adam told me about it, and the next day I called Myles, and we talked for a while. He said that just merely talking made him feel respected, wanted, loved, and mostly happy and peaceful. He said that for us to take the time to invest in him, for him, and to care so deeply, moved him. When he came to Big Sur the following week, something inside of him changed. He was open to coming to church with us, and what he found there was forgiveness, acceptance, joy, peace, love, hope, strength, and salvation. He told us that he found the meaning of grace and purpose and wanted to act upon it, live in it, understand it more, and continue to be open to embracing, believing, and living in this newfound life that he never knew before.

The music moved him, as did the messages, vibe, atmosphere, and the genuine care of the people.

Adam, Tara, Myles, and I went out to dinner the next night, and Myles told us that he hadn't talked to his family in a while. He resented his parents and they rarely spoke. He asked us if we thought that it would bring him closure or peace to reach out to them every so often. We spoke about the importance of family and also encouraged him to make the right decision, one that wouldn't cause more hurt or resentment. We told him that we would pray for him and encouraged him to pray about it too. He told us he would let us know the outcome.

When Myles went back home, he called Adam and told him that he joined a local church there and was currently in therapy as well with a Christian therapist. The program that he was in, as well as the people he found, were his support. He told him that those weights and chains that he felt before from depression were breaking every day. We told Myles that we would visit him in Nevada sometime. He was grateful. We kept in touch with him, and he shared that he joined a group at his church, which had been a strong blessing for him and an anchor in his life.

The next day, Adam was at his parents' house. He

filled Tara and I in on what happened with Dean's mom.

"Adam James," Tammy said. "I ran into Dean's mom at the store the other day. She had a lot to say about you. She was thankful that you helped Dean. She gave me a half apology too about all that stuff that she said about interracial relationships and race. You know we love Tara, and she brings you joy and to our family too. Keep her, Adam."

"I will, Mom. I love her. She's my best friend," he said. "So, what did she say to you Mom?"

"She said, 'You have a great son, and I know I said things before, but maybe it wasn't all what I thought it was.'"

"Okay, that's good. Sometimes people are like that, but I really don't care what they think about Tara and me."

"I know, sweetie. That's what makes me so proud of you. You don't let things bother you too much."

"Oh, Tara's calling now, Mom."

"Hello?"

"Hey Adam," she said. "My grandmother is really sick. My mom is with her now in the hospital, and my dad is on the way there now. My brother can't make it right now, but I am going to head over there too."

"Okay, I will come too," he said.

"Okay babe, thank you. Can you meet me at the hospital?"

Adam and Tara arrived at the hospital separately but close in time, with Tara arriving first. Adam met Tara in the hallway after checking in, and Tara ran into his arms. They hugged and embraced. Tears rolled down Tara's face.

"I hope she will be okay," Tara said.

"I hope so too. I know how close you two are, babe. I pray that she will be okay too."

Tara grabbed Adam's hand, and they met her family in the hospital room on the fifth floor. Her mom was in the room crying and holding on to her mother's hand. By her side was her husband (Tara's father), Tara's cousin, and her Aunt Cecilia, who is her mother's sister. Her husband was on his way. Her mother's brother was not able to make it, but he called in. There was also her Aunt Tatiana, her dad's sister, who is really close to her mother as well since the days when they all went to college together.

Tara's dad is three years older than her mom. Tara was sitting next to her mother with her head on her shoulder, and Adam was next to her, holding her hand.

"Mommy," Denise was saying as she held her mother's hand. Tara felt anxious, nervous, and scared. She could see that Adam also felt the same way, especially for her and her family. He also really cared for her grandmother, and they had a special, playful relationship. It was also sweet. She really liked Adam.

"Thank you for being here," Tara's father said to Adam. Her mom touched his arm and said thank you in a quiet voice as well.

The nurse came in and said that it wasn't looking too good for her grandmother in all honesty but that there is always a chance, so she couldn't really say for sure.

"I need some time," Tara said, and she and Adam went out into the hallway. "It's really hard, Adam, for me and for my mom to see her losing her mom and how that must feel. She's already lost her father."

"I know. When my dad's mom died, we weren't there. She was alone in the hospital, and we arrived after. That was hard. I saw it coming because, before, her vitals were low. It was a hard call to hear."

Adam has one set of grandparents left.

"Let's go back in the room," Tara said.

The family prayed, shared memories, stories, verses, songs, and ultimately watched her grandmother take her last breath. They were in the hospital room for an hour and a half to two hours until that moment.

Tara's mother fell to the floor crying when the nurse confirmed it by checking her vitals after she saw her take her last breath. She held to that momentary hope but knew she was gone.

Her father embraced her mother. "It will be okay, Denise," he said. "I'm sorry. She is out of pain. She is in heaven. She is in heaven," he repeated.

Aunt Cecilia sat holding on to her mother's hand, crying quietly. Tatiana was in the corner getting ready to hug them, and Tara sat there in disbelief and grief. It was a lot for her to process. It was also too much for her cousin.

Memories from her childhood to her adult life flooded her memory. She would knock on the door, and her grandma would say, 'Who is it?' in an excited, high-pitched voice, knowing that it was Tara. Moments where they ate popcorn and ice cream together because her grandma knew she liked it. Moments they would spend talking on the phone most days. Times when Tara would pick her up to go to church or go somewhere. All the trips and visits that they had together and the sound of her voice. All of the family gatherings and holidays, all of the sleepovers. It was all too much for her to bear. It was real.

Adam took her into his arms. Then he looked over at her mother crying hysterically on the floor on her knees, and he went over to embrace her. He softly said to her that he was so sorry and tried to console her. It was a hard night. None of them got much sleep.

Tara called me late that night to tell me everything. We talked about what it was like to be at this point of life when we are losing our grandparents. The walk from the hospital room to the car was a long and strange walk for all of them as they left her grandma. She said she'll never forget looking into the nurse's face and how that moment felt. We pondered life, meanings, situations, our body, and, most of all, time. Time can't be erased, fast-forwarded, or rewound. Time is right now, right here. Even when each day has similarities, it's a new day. They walked out with a bond that night. One of processing emotions of something intense that was seen and felt.

Adam and I felt for Tara, and we understood what loss like that was like. It was new being without. The arrangements were to follow. Tara kept me updated on everything and leaned on me for support, which I was glad to give her.

The next day, Adam and Tara were at Tara's parents' house, along with her aunts, Cecilia and Tatiana.

"Thank you for coming yesterday, Adam. It means a lot to us," Denise said.

"You got it, Ms. Denise," Adam said as he leaned in and hugged her.

"Yes, Adam, I know we don't know each other well, but I have heard nothing but good things about you from my niece and my sister," Cecilia said.

"He's the best," Tatiana said from a distance. "You guys might look like an unlikely couple—you have a lot of tattoos and Tara has none, you're White, she's Black—but I know your heart and hers, so I really like you, how you showed up for this family," said Tatiana.

"I appreciate it," Adam said.

"Plus, as a White man, you have been exposed to things that otherwise you would not have been, and I heard that you handled it very well," Tatiana said.

"I appreciate it. You guys are a great family, and I am

so blessed to know all of you and be taken in as one of your own," Adam said.

"You are always welcome in our family Adam," Cecilia said.

Tara's mom made them food and told Adam to make himself at home as always. They had heartfelt conversations throughout the day.

Later that night, Tara and Adam decided to go back to his house to watch a movie. They sat on his couch, and he looked at her with those sea bright, blue eyes. She melted in his eyes.

He could see it. "I love you, Tara Bear."

"I love you Adam James," she said back to him. "Thank you for everything, Adam."

He kissed her on the forehead.

His phone vibrated. "It's Myles. He was saying that he has been struggling lately with Tourette's syndrome."

"Oh wow," Tara said. "I had no idea that he had that."

"Yeah, it affects him, but he tries to hide it."

"That's sad," Tara said. "I know, I hope he will be okay. That's hard to deal with, and feeling ashamed of it could be a tough feeling to feel. We have to be thankful for what we have, every good health and function, you know. Never take it for granted. Others can have it worse."

"I agree, I am grateful every day," Tara said.

"I got you something, Tara Bear," Adam said as he reached behind him. It was a cute pink and red stuffed animal.

Tara leaned in, kissed Adam, and emphatically said thank you.

She asked him if he was seeing Derek tomorrow, and he told her that he was going to the gym with Derek and Branson if she wanted to come, as always, and that after they wanted to do a triple date with her, Monica, and me. Tara told him that it sounded good. She relayed it to me.

"Also, my sister is coming into town next week, so we can all hang out," Adam said.

"Aw, I love Jenny," she said. He kissed her on the cheek, and they watched a movie.

I was with my younger brother, who is funny, caring, and sweet at times. He is nineteen. He and I are close. We talk every day, and we enjoy each other's company, talking and hanging out. I know he looks up to me, loves me, and enjoys spending time together. He loves to joke around and be silly. I love being a good role model and example to him. He also defends and speaks up for me. He has that loyal, no one messes with my sister mentality, he'll take care of any issue from someone, and I love it. I care for him and love him too.

❧ Chapter 10

Adam's older sister, Jenny, arrived from South Dakota to their parents' house for a few days. Adam and Tara were there too. Jenny is thirty-two, with blonde hair that she sometimes dyes dark, blue eyes, a butterfly tattoo on her back, a flowery heart tattoo on her right wrist, and a positive tattoo quote on the back of her neck, right under her hair. The night started with a lot of laughter and good conversation. They made fun plans and reminisced on good times and time well spent. It was getting later into the night, and Adam's dad was working on something in his study, and his mom was also doing some work in her room. Adam, Tara, and Jenny sat together on the family room couch.

"Adam," Jenny said, "can Tara and I have some girl time? I don't get to see her much, but I love talking to her."

"I can't stay?" Adam asked playfully.

Jenny scrunched her face with a smile. "We have to talk about you, Adam."

"Okay, well don't talk too much," he said with a side smile. "Only good things."

Adam said he would go see what his dad was up to and text Branson.

Branson and I were together.

Jenny put her hand on Tara's lap for a second. "I am glad that you are doing well, Tara. You make Adam so happy, and my parents are always raving about you too."

"Aw, I love your family, Jenny."

"They are pretty great aren't they?" Jenny asked with a smile. The ladies laughed. "I love your family too, Tara. They are so open, kind, caring, supportive, and encouraging, and I know they are so good to Adam. Your dad is funny too, and your mom is so sweet. They both are."

"Aww yeah, for sure," Tara said. "So glad that we all talk and are all close with our families."

"You are such a gift and amazing addition to our family, and I am so thankful for you, Tara," Jenny said. "Not just the fact that you are great for and to Adam, just also who you are and how you reach out to me. I love hearing from you and all that you guys are up to. I hope that one day we will be sisters-in-law. I know my brother is going to ask you to marry him one day. I see the way he looks at you, and I hope when that day comes, you will say yes, because I just love you, and I love you for him. I can see how he feels about you in his eyes and when he puts his hand on your back when he's walking by, just in how he treats you. He thinks you are great; he admires you, and I know he loves you."

"Aw, thank you, Jenny. You have always treated me like family and included me. I appreciate you, and if he asked, I would be elated. He's my prince. I love him. He's amazing in so many ways, he's godly, handsome, caring, kind, good-hearted, fun, loving, and thoughtful. He always defends me and stands up for me, which is a quality that I like too. I couldn't not say yes to the best guy."

The ladies shared a tender moment and Jenny had an *aw sweet* expression on her face.

"So, how is South Dakota?" Tara asked her. "How's Dale?"

"It's good, and he's good. We have our adventures and projects that we are doing. Dale and I are enjoying it there, and as you know, his family is close by, my in-laws. My aunt, Dad's sister, is close by too, so that's been good.

"You know, Tara, I just want you to know something.

You and I talk, we text, and when I visit and you guys visit, we hang out, and we always have the best time. It's fun, carefree, and it's so refreshing. I love hanging out with you. Even having deep conversations together is great.

"I don't always talk too much about some stuff. I'm pretty private when it comes to my personal feelings with some people unless I know that I can really trust them and trust them not to judge me or hold it against me in the future. I just don't like second guessing what I say. I feel like I can trust you, Tara, just like with my family and friends. You are easy to talk to, understanding, open, and I know you're honest and have my best interest at heart when you say things and in the standards you have too, like Adam. I'm really into positive words and sayings. You've shared life changing things with me too.

"I'm big into telling people how you feel about them or that you love them. I make sure I do it with my family, my husband, and my friends. You and I have become friends, and being Adam's girlfriend, one day we could become family, and I just want you to always feel that sense of inclusion and unbiased support from me."

"That makes me feel really good," Tara said.

"I am thankful for you as a person, how you treat Adam with such love, and I know you let him lead and be the man that he is. You are so good for him and make him better," Jenny said.

"That means a lot to me, Jenny. Thank you for saying that. I really admire you. You're so nice, caring, and welcoming." The ladies smiled.

"Do you know someone who had a rocky road with their sister-in-law? Tara asked her.

"Yes, someone I met randomly, actually, who I was

able to help," Jenny said. "We met on a train, and we got to talking. We still reach out to each other. She went through a series of terrible situations with a lot of unkindness directed toward her, and this was a woman who was clearly caring, thoughtful, and undeserving of that treatment. She was treated meanly, given a hard time, and excluded from the beginning. The respect wasn't there even though she helped her sister-in-law, especially when asked. Her sister-in-law then made it seem like she never asked the woman certain questions or said certain things to her which made the woman help and share positive things. She also turned it around with lies and blame. She doesn't really know her, yet she often said rude things about her and misconstrued some things."

"I am sorry that happened to her. That's not a situation I'd envision before we met, and I am so glad that it's not our reality and that we are comfortable talking and being ourselves. Maybe it's jealousy. It sounds like the lady did nothing wrong and tried to approach her sister-in-law with open arms and kindness but was met with a mean spirit. I hope she knows that disconnect isn't her fault. It's on her sister-in-law and her own lack of character, not on her. It's normal to respond to disrespect but better to let the person just argue with themselves. People will see. That way too, you say less, and they may feel worse. It's interesting when people treat others badly 'cause if the treatment were reversed, she would probably be mad and not appreciate that. How could she expect more or for it to be different if roles were reversed at this point," Tara said.

Jenny nodded and said, "I agree, it's unacceptable and I know it has been hurtful to her and bothered her. It's been an unpleasant experience. In the beginning she thought they could have a rapport, share some general things, and talk, but since then, apart from being polite, she no longer wants to try much with her sister-in-law, doesn't have much to say, and doesn't see her in a good light or get a good vibe. Her sister-in-law has said unbelievable things, didn't apologize, and made lies up about things she said. She has also judged her differences and didn't want anything to do with her or care because of it and because of her perceived lack of all interests. She went looking for problems. There is certainly discord. I told the woman that of course she can always attend gatherings if she wants though; it is not up to her sister-in-law to say whether or not she can. The comfortability or interest from the lady isn't there for being more than at a distance though after all the rude things that have been said to her, and I get that especially when there are other things to do. The sister-in-law is set in her ways and it's not always peaceful, but the woman tries to have peace and be polite. She's a friendly person. She tries to keep quiet at received aggression instead of replying when she has to be there for her husband. She never started drama. Hearing about it all made me want to make it clear to you that I'm all about good vibes and friendship.

"I value, care for, and respect you and want you to always feel comfortable with me. I enjoy our bond and rapport. It's important to me as is being there for you as my future sister-in-law."

"I completely understand why she wouldn't be inclined or interested to try with her anymore after the bad behavior and how she was unfairly treated for no reason. Hopefully the sister-in-law can try to be decent and stop saying bad things about her. It sounds stressful. It's important to me too with you; I agree and feel the same way," said Tara.

"I want to be someone that you want to talk to and always be yourself. No judgment, no bringing stuff up later, no drama or fiddling problems that don't make sense, just genuine realness and if anything ever happened that maybe we misunderstood, I want to fix it, 'cause just as I love and care about Adam and am close with him, I want to have that bond and care with the love of my brother's life too, his life partner, the woman by his side," Jenny said.

"I appreciate you and your mere presence. I never want you to feel or have to wonder, *Does Jenny like me?* Because I know how that feels," Jenny said.

Tara looked at her with warmth and kindness. "Wow," Tara said. "Thank you for being so open with me and sharing how you feel. It's important for me to be friends with you too, and I think that you are the nicest, sweetest, kindest person. You are so fun and open. I am glad that you shared this and that we are continuing to build a great relationship. I always love and enjoy talking to you."

"It would be my loss if I didn't want that with you, Tara."

"I am so happy to hear you say all of this. Being warm and kind is important, and you exude that, Jenny," Tara said with a smile.

"Family is everything to me," Jenny said. "It's where life starts and love never ends. You being with Adam is an extension, and we have more love to give, girl."

"Having a future sister-in-law like you is what I imagined or hoped for, Jenny. I am so glad that we get along and that you care about me too and want to have that relationship with me personally. I think we understand each other well. It makes it all easier. When my brother gets a girlfriend then wife, I want to be to her what you are to me, Jenny, a great future sister-in-law. I hope we will get along and that she will be nice and have good qualities," Tara said.

"Aw, that is so sweet," Jenny said. "I am so glad that

we get along, and by default, your place in our family means something. I am so glad that you love the life you have with Adam and I thank you for loving and caring for my brother. Never let anything change that or affect what you two have. It is special. Keep enjoying it. Always be yourself."

Tara squeezed her hand. "Thank you for being so welcoming and being kind and inclusive. Family is everything to me too, and I am really close with my family. To have additional family in you guys is so nice too and important to me too to talk, share things, and have that consistently. I know I can trust you, even with personal things,"

"You are so smart, mature, and loving. You are a good person," Jenny said.

Tara thanked her.

"The depth of marriage is important to me. When you and Adam get married, you are family. I don't want to put any pressure on you, but I do hope that one day you will be more than his girlfriend and we can be sisters-in-law. I appreciate you, Tara, and you are really special to me and to our whole family. I see how Adam looks at you and feels about you and how you feel about him and look at him too. My parents love you."

"Thank you so much, Jenny," Tara said. "That really means a lot to me. I am blessed to be dating a guy with such a wonderful family who have genuinely accepted me and has taken me in, along with loving my family too."

"We all deserve that, Tara," Jenny said. The ladies shared a tender moment. The ladies miss each other when they are apart and also admire each other's beauty.

Adam walked by and saw them hugging. "Two of my favorite ladies," he said. He leaned on Jenny's shoulder and hugged her. "I am so glad that you are here with us, Jenny, and that we are all having a great time."

"Jenny," Tara said, "Our friend Lila and a couple other friends want to go to Florida coming up, and you should come!"

"I would love to. That would be so fun. Florida is beautiful, and Dale and I actually want to explore work opportunities there and consider moving there too or to Arizona. We might go there for his 36th birthday next month too."

"That's awesome," Tara said. Jenny told Adam and Tara that she was so thankful for them. Thankful to have a brother who is also a best friend and his girlfriend who is amazing and has become a friend to her. Tara reflected on what Jenny told her. She felt thankful that Adam's sister had such a kind and good heart. Tara and I texted the rest of the night and it warmed my heart to hear about this.

🌿 Chapter 11

The next day, Adam was at the gym with Branson. Someone that Adam met at the gym named Mosaic was there too working out with them.

"Adam, you're a Christian right?" Mosaic asked him.

"I am."

"Right, I knew you were different in a good way," Mosaic said. "I see the way you treat people. I see the way you are living with a standard of doing certain things and not doing certain things, whether it be with things you do, say, or listen to, or watch. I see it too from things you've said or that I've asked you. The way that you carry yourself and just your aura. It's very positive. I really admire that."

"I appreciate that, that means a lot," Adam said.

"I try to be good, but I'm looking for more, something greater than just me. I just want to say that you've been really cool to me. Different from the way some other people have treated me in general. They weren't of any faith, it's not that, they just weren't nice to me, and they made fun of my national origin," Mosaic said.

"You listen, I admire the things you share, and I admire the way that you live your life. Stick to those standards because I see that you're a great person living for God. I know some guys or people give you grief for it and make light of it, ridicule you, make jokes, and don't respect it or maybe even understand why you are set apart and not doing crazy things. But, for me, it's been refreshing to get to know you here at the gym and to see someone so genuine," Mosaic said.

"Thank you, Mosaic," Adam said. "That really means a lot. That is so nice of you to say. Thank God that through Him

I can make a difference and that you were blessed by it. At the end of the day, that's what matters. That's what counts."

Mosaic agreed and went on to tell Adam more. "Sometimes people say ignorant things, and when they group people together, or think they are all a certain way, oftentimes that is wrong, but they can't see that their mentality is the real problem.

"They sometimes can't see that the intolerance and unwillingness to understand is really within them not just from others. Sometimes people don't have all of the facts but assume things when, in fact, the opposite may be true or wrong if you really listen and look into it. Thinking about the meanings of things is important, as well as truly understanding and accepting," Mosaic said.

Just then, Derek arrived at the gym and greeted the group. He walked in macho with his gym bag. The guys worked out for a little while and Derek started getting into a verbal argument with another guy. It got heated and Derek and the guy were in each other's faces, threatening to fight. The shouting match started to get bad and caused a scene.

Adam put himself in between them and broke it up. He put his hand on Derek's chest. "You're better than this man. It's not worth it. Cool down. You're better than this. Just walk away. Cool down!"

Derek began to back up, grabbed his bag, and said that he was out of there.

Adam followed him out. "What happened, man?" He asked with his hands open.

"I don't like when people disrespect me," Derek told him. "Very disrespectful, that guy was."

Adam nodded. "It's hard, man, but sometimes it's just not worth it. You have a lot going for you, Derek. You don't want to throw that away bro. Don't mess that up."

"I just don't like when someone disrespects me, Adam."

"I get it. I've been there. I'll never forget the time that I reached out my hand to shake this guy's hand, and he didn't shake it back. He looked at me with disgust and as if I were nothing. I stood there humiliated in front of a lot of people. I felt like time stood still. I never felt so low as in that moment, almost like I wasn't a worthy person. I'm not ashamed of who I am in any way, but that disrespect brought me down at the time. I didn't let it define me though. Derek, you are better than this. I don't want to see you go down or get in trouble because someone else is in the wrong."

"Wow, man, that's messed up. Why did he not shake your hand?" Derek asked.

Adam shrugged. "He didn't shake it because I have a lot of tattoos, and he noticed them on my hands."

"I'm sorry, man," Derek said. "You're right. It's not worth jeopardizing what I've got going on for that guy. You know, Adam, you've experienced some stuff for having tattoos, and you're dating Tara, who has experienced some stuff for being Black. Have you guys experienced it a lot for being in a relationship together besides the time I was there?"

"Not really. People have been pretty accepting toward us."

"And for you dating a Black girl, has that been different?"

"No, I always saw Tara as a woman who I was getting to know and now who I am close to. We clicked early on, and our racial differences never hindered us or played into my feelings for her or how I saw her as my girlfriend. She's my best friend. When it comes to racism, I do see that. I want to support her through those things that obviously she can go through and be there for her."

"That's good. She's mentioned situations that were racist and having to deal with that. You guys deal with it similarly and differently at the same time. I get worked up," Derek said. "The beautiful thing with us and with people in general is that we are all different yet similar. Tara will tell you herself and tells me that I am more of a forgiving person or chill at times, and she is a very nice person but can remember things more or hold onto them more. She's not always quick to let things go when someone has wronged her or feel comfortable going on with that person. My sister is like that too after she has given a lot of chances. They are similar in some regards. Everyone handles things differently and approaches things how they feel most comfortable. Tara is into letting someone know how they were wrong sometimes and might bow out other times. I don't blame her," Adam said.

"You guys balance each other out well; you're a great couple and always supported Monica and me," Derek said.

"Thank you. We love you guys. It can be hard when you've been mistreated. I've learned a lot from Tara on many things. She's smart and has a lot of great attributes. I wouldn't want to be with anyone else."

Derek agreed. "You're a good guy, Adam. We've got nothing but love for you and Tara. From the day I met you, I've learned a lot from you too and have had fun. I have a lot of tattoos too, and I'm a big Black dude, so I get it. Mine are darker than yours, just being that I am darker."

"Yeah, you know, the guy who didn't want to shake my hand later found out who my dad was, because it was his office party, and he apologized to me for judging me," Adam said. "I accepted the apology, and he shook my hand. When he heard that I was Chuck's son, and when my dad's colleague introduced us, I could see the embarrassment and surprise on his face from how he treated me earlier when I tried to greet him. It's funny too because the next day I was going to get a new tattoo done."

"Should have shown him that fresh open wound the next day, be like, you don't like my tats, well, I'm getting another one tomorrow," Derek said. "Better yet, come to the tattoo shop and see it get done. See the needles inject ink into my skin that makes these designs."

Adam smiled.

"Man, how do you deal with these people though?" Derek asked.

"Turning the other cheek is hard, Derek, and loving your neighbor like you love yourself is hard when your neighbor is hard to love."

"How do you do that? How do you forgive and let go?" Derek asked.

"I had to decide who I wanted to be. The Adam who follows that Bible verse, the Adam who follows the God of the Bible, or the Adam who stays stuck or consumed in the weight of burdens because sometimes people aren't their best. Just pray for them. For me, I want to rise above and not let people's actions determine how I am. I know who I am. I want to be more like Jesus even though it can be hard.

"I'm used to some people judging me for what's on my skin rather than just getting to know me first for who I am or making assumptions about me. Some of them might be true for some people, but a lot aren't. I don't really have a gnarly past, for example. Tattoos are visual but there's more to me on the inside too, just like with you or with anyone.

"For me, I want to be a man of my word, do what I

say, say and do what I mean, and exemplify that. Be honest and treat people the way that I want to be treated. I want to be someone who people can count on and trust. Someone who follows God. That's who I strive to be every day, and every day I can improve and get better, 'cause no one is perfect.

"I am grateful and blessed to know you, Derek. We've had good conversations that made us think, and we relate on so many things. I don't want to see you fall or go down because someone else has a problem. It seems like it's always the one who retaliates when they are wronged that can end up being viewed as wrong because the provocative act by others may not be witnessed."

"Thank you, Adam," Derek said. "You're real, bro, and I appreciate that. I used to care too much what people thought at times or felt like this or that, but just like you, I am pretty confident and happy with where I am now. I want to trust God more. I know we can let go and give it to Him," Derek said.

"You exude confidence, Derek," Adam said.

Derek laughed and thanked Adam for being a good friend.

"Another good thing about you is that you are open to exposing yourself to different people, which helps to not see those differences as much, or at least not in a bad way," Derek said.

Adam nodded in agreement.

The guys filled us in on what happened when we all met up.

The next day, Adam arrived at Tara's house dressed up and looking spiffy. She opened the door, and he met her there with flowers behind his back. He gave it to her and gave her that smile that he has that always melts her. She blushed, hugged him, and thanked him wholeheartedly. She loves when he does those cute surprises and brings her favorite snacks and flowers and creates a romantic atmosphere.

"Do you want to go to the overlook?" he asked her. They went, and the view was breathtaking. The waves crashed on the shore below. There were palm trees, pine trees, live oak trees, and cypress trees in view. They sat there on a rock with a blanket together on their shoulders.

"Babe, can I talk to you about something?" she asked him.

"Anything," he said.

"Sometimes I have these moments when I cry, and I think about calling my grandma. Sometimes I think of something that I want to tell her, just wanting to talk to her, ask her for advice, or remember the times that we had. Those moments and memories of seeing her, whether it was at her house, my house, visits, talks, picking her up for church, or somewhere where we would go often come to me.

"Sometimes that feeling comes and is replaced with the one that I will not be able to call her and talk to her. It's just gone. It's over. I can't believe she is gone. Sometimes I dream about it that she's still here. Time keeps going, the years go on, we get older, year after year. I am so thankful for the times that we had though."

"I know things have been hard. Think about all the amazing memories that you had together and for the person that she was to you. You had a special bond, and I know that the person you were to her was someone really special to her. She loved you and looked forward to your calls and visits. It's okay to cry it out. It's hard. Lila would say the verse, 'Faith shows the reality of what we hope for and assurance of what we don't see.' I hope that you will see her again someday, Tara, and that she knows how you feel. That bond is unbreakable. I'm always here for you."

She thanked him and then leaned on his shoulder. He smiled at her. She told him that what she learned and did was to embrace the moment in the moment, 'cause once that point in time is gone, one day it will be a memory that you can't get back.

"How's Jenny doing?" Tara asked him. "Did you talk to her today?"

"Yes, I talked to her this morning. She's good. She's home."

"Jenny is so welcoming and kind to me. I love her. Sometimes, with people at work, or other people, it can be hard to deal with hostile people or feel left out. Even if someone doesn't verbalize something, you can tell through their actions how they feel. If they ignore you, don't hold the door, don't say anything when they see you, look down and look like they have a sullen face or bad attitude, that speaks volumes too.

"I don't like being around people like that, especially when it's for a stupid reason or something that they don't want to let go of. Something that wasn't a big deal. Sometimes people make things up just to make themselves feel better or try to come up with all of these bad things about someone that come out of left field or are unbeknownst to them. I just try to remind myself about the people who do love and like me and the wonderful things they think and say about me. They see my character and who I am, not this made-up version of who they want to see that maybe is just a reflection of the bad person that they are," Tara said.

Adam kissed her cheek. "Babe, it's hard, but try not to worry about these people. The significance of the words that they speak are not indicative of the person that you are. It's indicative of the person that *they* are. It's insignificant even if it doesn't feel like that. Who cares what they think. It doesn't matter. They aren't your family, your friends, or people that will go through life with you in that way. If they want to bring you down, they are the one with the problem. Or if they want to treat you like that and make up stupid reasons to not like you, accuse you of stupid things that they feel you did to them or not, they are the problem, not you. Sometimes people do hurtful and stupid things too for no reason, and then either don't realize or don't care that they are in the wrong. It upsets me when people upset you and when you are upset, babe, and as hard as it is, you have to try to not let it get to you for your health and peace. Think of those who revere and see you."

"I know. When I'm away from them it's fine, but when I have to see them, it's annoying," Tara said.

"I know, babe," Adam said. "Tara, you have so much going for you, so many strong qualities, and people who love you and think you are special and great. Those people who don't, don't have good taste. They are being blocked for something on them."

"Thank you, babe. You always know how to make me feel better," Tara said with a soft smile.

"It's true. You have changed my life for the better. You make me want to be better. I was telling Derek the other day when he was asking about you and we talked about personality and how we all handle things. Our differences and similarities make us who we are, and we work well together," Adam said.

"Oh, definitely, we always talk about that," Tara said.

"You never cease to amaze me, and I love how deeply we're connected. No one can take who you really are away from you. If they don't see how amazing you are for so many reasons and in so many ways, it's on them."

"Thank you, babe. You always speak with such eloquence," Tara said.

"This weekend, do you want to meet up with Branson, Lila, Derek, and Monica?"

"Yeah, that would be really fun," Tara said. "We can do some bike riding, swimming, go out to eat, and go see some live music at night."

Adam agreed that would make for a great weekend.

The next day, Adam and Tara were off, and they were going to a ballet and acrobat show with Adam's parents and his aunt, Janine. After that, they were going to go over to her parents' house to hang out and do some stuff with them. They had a gala to attend with them the next day and were also going to go with them to the park to do some exercise and maybe the beach beforehand.

Adam and Tara were at his parents' house, and his dad was telling him how proud of him he was. Chuck looked at his son. "Adam, I am so proud of you," he said. "Your mom and I always have been. From the time you were little to now being an adult, you have always amazed us, been adventurous and fun, loving, kind, caring, and always beating to your own drum."

"Thanks, Dad, that means a lot."

"It's true," his dad said. "The man you've become and always have been, makes us proud, and we are proud and happy that you have Tara by your side. She complements you well and is really good for you. She's the best. We love her family too, and we know that they feel the same way about you."

Branson and I went out for dinner and then we joined them at the house and enjoyed a wonderful evening together.

Chapter 12

I'll never forget the day that I met Adam because it was a day that my eyes were opened. I wondered how Adam thought I saw him when it came to his tattoos. It was a day that led to a series of events and adventures. Little did I know all that it would entail. I made best friends in Adam and Tara. Through him I met Branson.

My purpose was to learn and grow by knowing others, by hearing their life stories and being there for them. It made me better. If I could help or make a difference for someone, even just for one, then it's worth it. To be a light in the dark is worth it. Together we were able to help the people we met with genuine care.

De La Lina brought us all together, but love kept us together. So again, I wondered, why are there stereotypes? Why are people sometimes so mean and critical? I wrote in my journal. Seeing past exterior looks and into who someone is, was something people even learned from us. We challenged perceptions and imaginations. The way that everyone handled conflicts that got thrown their way taught me too. I think about my story, our story. I'm still a rebel with a cause.

At his house, Adam, Tara, and I talked about Jesus. We all attend church. Tara attended her whole life, so did I, and Adam started attending weekly in his mid-twenties. Before that, he grew up going to church occasionally with his family, but it was infrequent. It wasn't something that was a big part of his growing up but was something that they did sometimes, which they thought was a good thing to do.

We grew up in youth groups and went to church programs on different days of the week. The talks, the music bands, singers, the events, the programs, the people, it all shaped us into who we are. Tara also grew up going to a small and close-knit Christian school, which she loved. She built connections and played sports there. We talked about how ultimately, for us, it is Jesus's love for us that gives us the hope, strength, and motivation to be who we are. It's because of Him that we want to be who we are and be and do better in how we live in our actions and lives.

Tara said that she wants to grow more in where she is with her faith and her walk. She strives to be more like Him and have her heart break for things that break His heart; loving God and loving people. It reminded me of the verse that says to "Do justice, love mercy, and walk humbly with God." Some people may not understand or want to hear it, and it could be a sore subject for some, an interesting subject for others, a curious one and an agreeable one for others. There are misconceptions about our faith sometimes, but ultimately, I learned so much from knowing Tara and Adam. I learned so much from being myself.

They say that I inspired them to be better, to think more critically, more Biblically, to be like Christ, to act more lovingly, but I learned from them too. I saw the way they were even when they were hurt and helped people who were even more hurt or broken, or maybe they were just hurt and broken in a different way. I saw the perseverance in Tara. I saw the good in Adam's heart that day in the hospital and time and time again. The way he handled things at the concert and with Sean, Jason, and everyone moved me. Being close to Tara and sharing a bond and conversations blessed me, being able to be there for her and her for me. She is pure joy, just like her middle name.

Knowing Branson through Adam is one of my greatest blessings, and Branson since asked me to be his girlfriend. We are going strong, and our families love each other. He's amazing.

He loves learning about my culture. The greatest commandment and the ones thereafter will always be mine to cling to. Pulling from the Bible, "With faith, hope and love, love is the greatest above all. Without it, speaking in the tongues of angels is just resounding noise."

Everything and everyone have shaped me along the way, but I owe it to God and to my family. My path is made straight by the God of hope, so I take hope from the one who overcame. I am so grateful for it all. If I could tell my younger self one thing or see it then, it would be dream big. The future is yours. Oh, the places we'll go, the things we'll see, and the people we'll know. It's good to get out and see the world. There is more. I still have questions, but I've gotten answers. It's a journey. I penned words to paper in my journal. If I could share something with someone, I would say that when you feel you need to say or do something to help someone or have the moment or opportunity to make a difference or speak out, take it, because that day, that moment, that point in time, you may never get it back. It could be just for that day, the meaning in that specific day and point in time, day by day, that wouldn't be the same another day. Each day is special. Be thankful. Don't worry too much about what others think. See the bigger picture. 1 John 4:4 and Ezekiel 37:1-14 are verses that stuck with me. My parents text me Bible verses, devotionals, and giphys, and words of encouragement every morning. They sustain me and give me hope and strength. Those verses were answers of promise to my prayers. In any situation I know that there can be restoration as the Bible says, "Dry bones hear the word of the Lord." God said live. I've seen it. I've heard it. I know that "Greater is he who is within me than he who is in the world." Knowing that, I can stand through any obstacle. I wrote it all in my journal as I reflected. For such a time as this. This journey is to be continued.

The End

🌿 Author's Note

I want to thank God firstly for giving me the ideas created in my head and the desire to write this book. I've always been a dreamer and I am thankful. I think back to the 12-year-old me and me throughout the years, singing in my music room, writing, and dreaming.

I am thankful to the people who just by being themselves unknowingly inspired me to write this book from bits and pieces of things I have seen, heard, and just ideas that came to my mind to make a story. It's a blessing making up ideas in my mind to create a story.

Thanks to my editors from Reedsy and my incredible book designer for making this book, the cover and bringing my ideas to life. I am thankful for the time, effort and patience spent on this book and on this process.

Big thanks to my husband, Russell, for listening to my ideas, listening to me talking about my characters like they are real people that I know and love, my questions about my story, reading over the book a few times, your input and helping me to make this book the best that it can be. We've worked hard on this book. I love our time together always, every adventure and experience. Thanks for being there.

Thank you very much to my parents for all of the encouragement, support and love always. Thanks for being proud of me. You have both shaped me and taught me so much. I had an amazing childhood as you know, with countless dear memories and it's a great life. Thanks for everything. I love our time together, all our talks and experiences. I love my endearing and sweet nicknames. Writing doesn't fall far from the tree.

I want to thank my brother, Moise, for the support and enthusiasm in helping with marketing this book and believing in it. Thank you so much. I was so happy to get a little brother. I've loved growing up with you. I love our time together and adventures.

I am thankful for all of the educational and sports experiences I've had and the people along the way.

Thank you to my High School Tenth Grade Honors English teacher for inspiring and encouraging us to get our poems published and for telling us about it. I'll never forget it.

Thank you to all of my family and friends for the support! I really appreciate you all.

Last but not least, thank you to all of you who purchased this book and are reading it, for making this a reality. I hope that this story inspires you, makes you think and that you thoroughly enjoy it. I hope it touches you and that parts of it make you laugh too. I hope you see yourself in at least one of the characters and imagine life through a different lens. Enjoy it from start to finish with all of the twists and turns as you get to know Lila, Adam, Tara, Monica, Derek, Branson and others.

✿ About the Author

M.N. Walters has always enjoyed writing from the time that she was a child. She would write stories, songs, and has had poems published. M.N. is passionate about storytelling and putting ideas to paper to share and inspire others. She has an interest in creating thoughts and ideas and bringing them to life. This is M.N. Walters debut novel. She has a Bachelor's degree in Psychology: Human Services and a Masters degree in School Counseling. When she is not writing and working, M.N. can be found relaxing and enjoying the sun at the pool, sitting outside on the balcony, going to the beach, and walking and biking in nice scenery at paths and parks. M.N. also enjoys attending and being involved in her church, going to live music downtown, listening to music and watching shows and movies. She also enjoys going to nice places, sightseeing, spending time with family and friends, and exploring locally as well as traveling. M.N. was born and raised in New Jersey and is Jamaican. She lives in Florida with her husband.

The Valley of Dry Bones

Ezekiel 37:1-14

37 The hand of the Lord was on me, and he brought me out by the Spirit of the Lord and set me in the middle of a valley; it was full of bones. 2 He led me back and forth among them, and I saw a great many bones on the floor of the valley, bones that were very dry. 3 He asked me, "Son of man, can these bones live?"

I said, "Sovereign Lord, you alone know."

4 Then he said to me, "Prophesy to these bones and say to them, 'Dry bones, hear the word of the Lord! 5 This is what the Sovereign Lord says to these bones: I will make breath[a] enter you, and you will come to life. 6 I will attach tendons to you and make flesh come upon you and cover you with skin; I will put breath in you, and you will come to life. Then you will know that I am the Lord.'"

7 So I prophesied as I was commanded. And as I was prophesying, there was a noise, a rattling sound, and the bones came together, bone to bone. 8 I looked, and tendons and flesh appeared on them and skin covered them, but there was no breath in them.

9 Then he said to me, "Prophesy to the breath; prophesy, son of man, and say to it, 'This is what the Sovereign Lord says: Come, breath, from the four winds and breathe into these slain, that they may live.'" 10 So I prophesied as he commanded me, and breath entered them; they came to life and stood up on their feet—a vast army.

11 Then he said to me: "Son of man, these bones are the people of Israel. They say, 'Our bones are dried up and our hope is gone; we are cut off.' 12 Therefore prophesy and say to them: 'This is what the Sovereign Lord says: My people, I am going to open your graves and bring you up from them; I will bring you back to the land of Israel. 13 Then you, my people, will know that I am the Lord, when I open your graves and bring you up from them. 14 I will put my Spirit in you and you will live, and I will settle you in your own land. Then you will know that I the Lord have spoken, and I have done it, declares the Lord.'"

1 John 4:4

"You, dear children, are from God and have overcome them, because the one who is in you is greater than the one who is in the world."